THE POCKET BOOK OF VAASTU

A PRACTICAL GUIDE

RAKESH CHAWLA

HIND POCKET BOOKS
An imprint of Penguin Random House

HIND POCKET BOOKS

USA | Canada | UK | Ireland | Australia
New Zealand | India | South Africa | China | Singapore

Hind Pocket Books is part of the Penguin Random House group of companies whose addresses can be found at global.penguinrandomhouse.com

Published by Penguin Random House India Pvt. Ltd
4th Floor, Capital Tower 1, MG Road,
Gurugram 122 002, Haryana, India

Penguin Random House India

First published in Hind Pocket Books by Penguin Random House India 2019
This edition published in 2022

10 9 8 7 6 5 4 3 2

The views and opinions expressed in this book are the author's own and the facts are as reported by him which have been verified to the extent possible, and the publishers are not in any way liable for the same.

ISBN 9789353493431

Printed at Manipal Technologies Limited, India

www.penguin.co.in

FSC www.fsc.org MIX Paper | Supporting responsible forestry FSC® C043100

This is a legitimate digitally printed version of the book and therefore might not have certain extra finishing on the cover.

HIND POCKET BOOKS

THE POCKET BOOK OF

VAASTU

A PRACTICAL GUIDE

An alumni of Modern School and St.Stephens College, Delhi, Mr. Rakesh Chawla feels he was destined to be a Vaastu proponent. It was during his tenure with Philips India that he was introduced to Vaastu Shastra in 1988. Since the past 20+ years, he has been refining and redefining the subject to make it easy to follow for the lay reader.

Contents

Foreword by *Bejan Daruwalla*

Om Shri Ganeshaya Namah

Vaastu is the ancient science of house building that has once again become very popular. I am not an authority on this subject like my friend Rakesh, who has explained it in this book in plain and simple language. He has actually made it easy to understand and now you can derive the maximum benefit of this knowledge from this practical book.

Both Astrology and Vaastu are derived from the Vedas. They are based on universal elements and seek to harmonize these elements which exist both within us and in our environment. Whereas astrology tracks the movements of planets and their energies in the form of a horoscope, Vaastu looks at the effect of elements and their energies in the form of the Vaastu Mandal.

In astrology the effect of planets as they move from one house to the other is different for each individual, whereas in Vaastu the directions are universal for each human being.

No doubt the knowledge from both the disciplines can be very useful even when applied together. In this book Rakesh has explained the various aspects of using the principles of Vaastu in residences, offices and plots without actually having to a hire a consultant.

May Ganesha shower his blessings on the author for his effort in simplifying such a complex subject.

Bejan Daruwalla

Preface

The importance and usefulness if Vaastu has once again been well understood in the modern world of today. Ten years ago when I started out it was quite a forgotten subjects and it was almost by accident that I entered this field.

When I was in handling sales in a multi national company, some suggestions were made to me by a religious person who visited my home. I made the changes but did not take the matter seriously.

Suddenly my career zoomed, I got tremendous recognition and also booked the biggest order ever for my company. When I reflected on events I somehow felt that the Vaastu suggestions made by my friend played a critical role in my change of fortune. I left my marketing career in 1991 and became a professional Vaastu consultant in 1994.

Since then I have witnessed many cases that have convinced me the efficacy of Vaastu. I recall the case of a dance teacher who requested me to help him as every aspect of his life seemed to be going wrong. His personal life was a mess, he had recently had an accident, and his health was slipping.

I went to his modest one room apartment and suggested he change the direction of his bed, and shift his cooking range and air conditioner. Over a period of a year dramatic changes occurred in his life!

Another case that comes to my mind is a family of garment exporters in the Okhla Industrial area of south Delhi. Everything seemed to be going well till they shifted their office to a much larger location.

Then suddenly there was a downslide. Payments got held up and there was domestic trouble as well. I suggested they relocate their cabin. I had also noticed a tree that was blocking the entrance to their gate, which I asked them to remove. Just these changes made a tremendous impact on their lives.

There was yet another case of an executive whose bedroom on the first floor faced a spearing land (a T-junction). In addition, his kitchen burner was under a beam. I suggested he shift his bed, and place an arrow directed towards the T-junction.

Within a year he received a double promotion to become Vice President Marketing of a multinational, and also received an overseas assignment.

However, I would strongly underline that mere arrangement and rearrangement of physical objects will not achieve the desired results. One's heart and spirit must be pure and so a deep commitment to right living is required.

As Swami Chinmayanand ji has said, "Living the right values of life is like building a dam across a river."

I take this opportunity to thank Poonam and Shekhar Malhotra of Hind Pocket Books for inspiring me to write this book. I would also like to send my best wishes to my readers, and urge them to read the book with an attitude of faith. It is then that the book will yield them the maximum benefit.

Rakesh Chawla

Institute of Vaastu Kala
H-91 Connaught Place
New Delhi
Phone : 3320972, 3320947
e-mail: vaastukala@hotmail.com
web: www.vaastuwisdom.com

Chapter One

WHAT IS VAASTU

Vaastu is a vast, ancient and complex wisdom as expounded in the Vedas. Traditionally, Vaastu *shastra* (*shastra* means treatise) covers all aspects of the science of building. It views the physical environment as an expression of the cosmic spirit. Thus, a building is, in essence, a recreation of the cosmos. As such, the direction of the building, the relationship between the building and its environment, the energies that will enter its spaces, the shape of the chosen plot, soil conditions — all these are dealt with in detail in the Vaastu *shastras*.

These *shastras* also contain numerous rituals which enhance our relationship to the earth and its energies. They also help us understand how intimately we are connected to the physical and spiritual environment.

The word *vaastu* is derived from the root *vas* which means 'to live' or 'to reside'. So Vaastu, in essence, deals with much more than architecture. It is about the art of living, in all its fullness, in accordance with a holistic view of life, where man is deeply connected to the universe and the energy of the elements.

Vaastu blends the psychological (our *vaasnas* or deep rooted desires) with the philosophical (the *vaastava* — the continuum or reality where resides our soul). It is in the blending of these two levels of human existence, and in its deep commitment to right living that the power of Vaastu lies.

Indeed, to see the material, psychological and spiritual as different aspects of one reality has been the world view of all ancient civilizations. In China, for example, Feng Shui has been practised for centuries by the rich and poor alike, and is integral to Chinese culture. Feng Shui, meaning 'wind and water', is based on the Chinese understanding of the dynamic flow of energy throughout the universe, and strives to maintain a proper balance between the forces of nature, just as Vaastu does. The fact that Vaastu is enjoying a spectacular revival bears testimony to its validity in today's world.

Similarly, the ancient Egyptians knew how to harness energy waves using the pyramid, in such a way that this unique energy affected the living and the dead elements stored within the pyramid. Today 'pyramid power' is being put to diverse uses such as storing fruits, vegetables and grains, and to enhance mental and physical well-being.

The goal of Vaastu is to enhance the well-being of the occupants of a building. It does so by ensuring that the plot is fully energised, and the building is in harmony with the cosmic elements. However, Vaastu does not make the claim that you will have no problems at all. It ensures that by creating a harmonious space you will be able to face the difficulties of life without much negativity.

The benefits of Vaastu are many. At the physical level, it provides comfort and convenience, and a user friendly environment that is full of space and light. At the psychological level, because of the aesthetic environment it creates, there is a feeling of well-being. Tensions lessen and relationships improve.

At the spiritual level, a person's sense of harmony deepens, and there arises an urge to understand the meaning of life and death. In fact, meditation and prayer contribute greatly to enhancing the positive vibrations that Vaastu creates.

With Vaastu, we are not changing our destiny. We are only trying to smoothen our life by making it more harmonious and thereby having peace of mind. Destiny always prevails, but by using remedial measures as provided by Vaastu, one can reduce the difficulties of one's life. Therefore, it is advisable to follow Vaastu to open the gates to a healthy, happy and prosperous life.

Chapter Two

PRINCIPLES OF VAASTU

According to Vaastu, the universe is full of beneficial energies which we must learn to harness as well as keep in balance if we wish to experience a state of well-being. Essentially, energy emanates from two chief sources — the elements (Space, Air, Fire, Water, Earth) and the electro-magnetic energy generated by the rotation of the earth.

Energy of the elements

An expression of the harmonious and dynamic interaction of the elements is the Natural Cycle. Water from the Earth evaporates into the atmosphere due to the heat in our solar system (sun). These droplets of water accumulate to form clouds. The air which moves the clouds makes them release the excess water which comes back to our planet in the form of rain. Thus the Cycle, as well as the equilibrium of the elements, is maintained on our planet.

To achieve this, the sun shines gloriously radiating warmth and light, the ocean offers itself to become vapour, the clouds condense into rain to quench the thirst of the parched earth, and

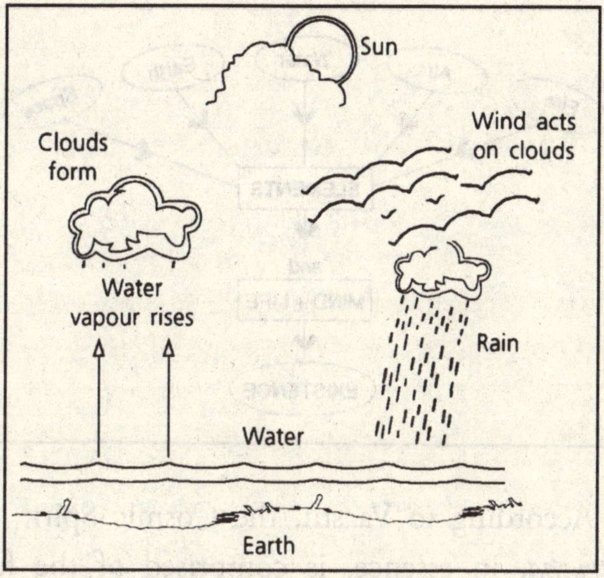

The Natural Cycle

the earth opens its body to nourish all beings. Thus, the universe offers itself unconditionally for our benefit, and is viewed by the Vedas as an expression of unconditional love.

To experience the Natural Cycle you need a mind, and to have a mind you need life. Therefore, the five elements and Mind and Life (see the diagram below) are the cause of our existence and must be kept in balance.

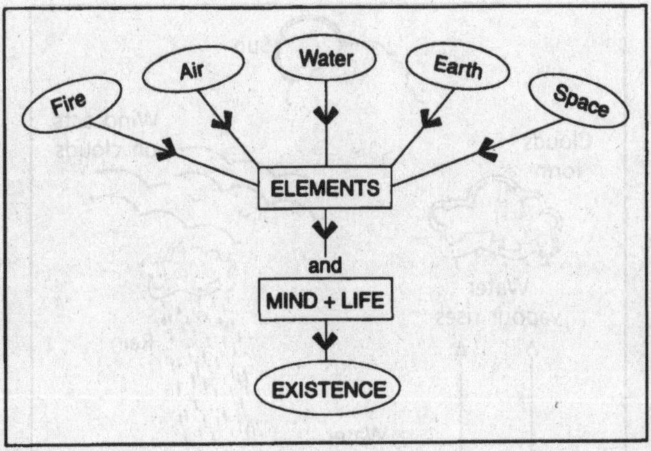

According to Vaastu, the Cosmic Spirit, or *Purusha,* in essence, is comprised of the five elements — earth, water, fire, air and space, and their origin is God. In Hindi, we address the Almighty as *Bhagvan,* where *Bh* stands for *bhoomi* (earth), *g* for *gagan* (space), *v* for *vayu* (air), *a* for *agni* (fire) and *n* for *neer* (water).

Therefore, the manifestation of Bhagvan (God) in the physical form is our universe.

Indeed, both within and without there is nothing but the elements. Our bodies are more than 60 percent fluids. Without air we would die. Our digestive fire creates energy by breaking down food, and the element earth is present in the bones and minerals within us. Our bodies absorb energy from food and the elements, but subtle energy, such as electro-magnetic energy, is absorbed through energy centres within us known as *chakras.* For more on *chakras,* see Chapter 13.

Elemental energy proceeds from subtle (space) to gross (earth), and in doing so, each successive element contains the properties of the preceding element.

SPACE is made of space alone.

AIR is made of space and air.

FIRE is made of space, air and fire.

WATER is made of space, air, fire and water.

EARTH is made of space, air, fire, water and earth.

Each element has its own attribute (*guna*) that is perceived by a sense organ. For instance, from fire emerges light and the receptor is our eyes. From air emerge feelings and the receptor is our skin. From earth emerges smell and the receptor is our nose. From water emerges taste and the receptor is our tongue. And from space emerges sound and the receptor is our ears. Here we see the link between the macrocosm (the universe) and the microcosm (the human being).

FIVE ELEMENTS	FUNCTION	SENSE ORGANS
FIRE	SIGHT	EYES
AIR	FEELING	SKIN
SPACE	SOUND	EARS
EARTH	SMELL	NOSE
WATER	TASTE	TONGUE

The cosmic link

In addition, each element generates its own form of energy as shown in the following chart.

ELEMENT	FORM OF ENERGY
FIRE	SOLAR
AIR	WIND
WATER	RAIN
EARTH	GRAVITATIONAL/MAGNETIC
SPACE	SOUND

Secondary energy sources

Electro-magnetic energy

Electro-magnetic energy flows along what is called the magnetic axis of the earth. This is an imaginary line between the North and South Pole along which these energy currents flow.

Electro-magnetic energy (*jeevika urja*) is created by the earth's rotation on its axis. Together, electro-magnetic energy and solar energy (*pranic urja*) sustain life on earth. Should the earth stop rotating on its axis, all life on earth would come to a standstill.

Vaastu Purusha Mandala

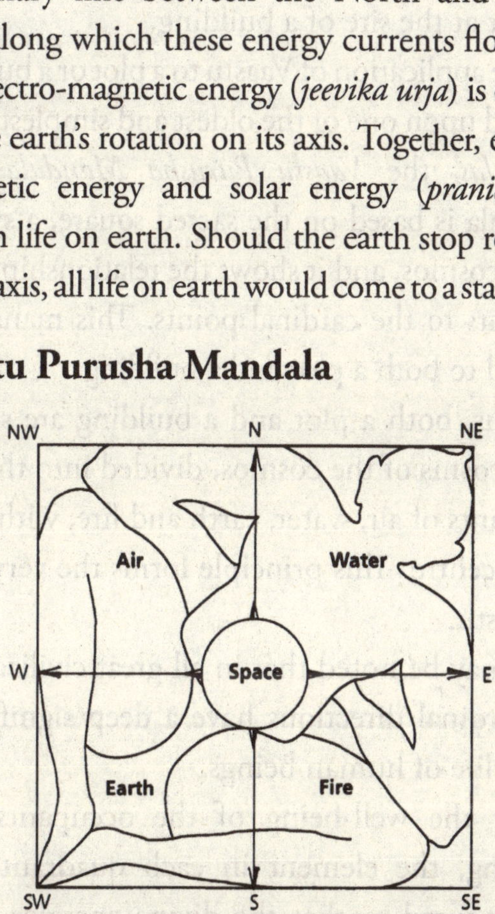

The basic Vaastu Purusha Mandala

In the Vedas, the *Purusha* is the inherent energy of the cosmos. Since one of the meanings of the word Vaastu is 'building site', *Vaastu Purusha* is taken to mean — the subtle energy present at the site of a building.

The application of Vaastu to a plot or a building is based upon one of the oldest and simplest Vedic *mandalas,* the *Vaastu Purusha Mandala.* This Mandala is based on the sacred square, a symbol of the cosmos, and it shows the relationship of the elements to the cardinal points. This mandala is applied to both a plot and a building.

Thus, both a plot and a building are seen as microcosms of the cosmos, divided into the four quadrants of air, water, earth and fire, with space at the centre. This principle forms the very basis of Vaastu.

It may be noted that in all great civilizations, the cardinal directions have a deep significance to the life of human beings.

For the well-being of the occupants of a building, the element in each quadrant must be honoured so that the divine energies of the cosmos are propitiated. In addition, the elements must be kept in balance as this creates powerful and beneficial energies which draw health, wealth and prosperity towards us.

On the other hand, an imbalance of the elements can create negative energies which maybe harmful.

The directions most suitable for different elements according to Vaastu are listed below:

The North-East (NE) quadrant is assigned to water. It is the appropriate place for a borewell, a pond, or an underground water tank.

The South-East (SE) quadrant is assigned to fire. Your kitchen, pantry, furnace or boiler should be placed there.

The North-West (NW) quadrant is assigned to air. The property of air is movement, so it is a good place to keep finished goods as they will move fast. If your guest room is located there, guests are not likely to stay for long.

The South-West (SW) quadrant is assigned to earth. It is the most stable of all the elements, so use this area as much as possible.

The Centre is assigned to space. This is a sacred area. Keep it empty and free of heavy furniture so that beneficial energies can circulate freely.

Just as an imbalance of the elements within our body creates discomfort and disease (this is studied deeply in Ayurveda), similarly an imbalance of elements in the natural cycle creates natural calamaties like typhoons, volcanic eruptions, floods etc. Likewise, an imbalance of the elements in our living environment disturbs our energy centres or *chakras.* We feel stressed and tense while our energies get dissipated in different directions.

Given below are the effects of the imbalance of elements in our immediate environment:

Earth. This element is connected with survival issues. An imbalance of this element, for example, a depression in the south-west, a water source in the south-west, or the south-west corner being cut off, can lead to loss of control in your business, health or family.

Water. This element is for procreation. An imbalance, like the north-east being raised or having a heat source, or the north-east being cut off, can restrict the expansion in business (especially finances) as well as the family.

Fire. This element is for vision and fame. An imbalance, such as a depression in the south-east or the existence of a water source in the south-east, can hinder prosperity and bring a bad name to business and family. It can also create conflict.

Air. This element is for feelings. An imbalance, like a water source in the north-west, a depression in the north-west, or the north-west being more elevated than the south-west, can block the feelings of people towards you, your products, your services and also increase your expenses.

Space. This element is for internal strength. An imbalance, like the centre of your establishment being depressed or having a water source, or something heavy being stored there, can cause you to lose inner strength and can also cause a drain in your finances.

When our peace of mind is disturbed, we have to redirect our energies subjectively as well as objectively, and meditation is the most effective method of doing this. Meditation creates positive energy and helps to accelerate the process of energy flow, and the good effects of this are then felt in our lives. For more on meditation, see Chapter 13.

CHECK LIST

Do you face any of these problems?

- *Financial problems.* Investigate the north-east of your house/office. Clean the clutter.
- *Relationship problems.* Check the west and north-west of your house/office. Clear the junk and keep a photo of your loved one there. Check the position of your bedroom (see pg. 77).
- *Health problems.* Check the east and south-east of your house/office, and keep a healthy plant there. Check the position of your kitchen (see pg. 83).
- *Insecurity.* Check the south and south-west of your house/office, and have plenty of light in that area. Check the position of your cabin in the office (see pgs. 110-114).
- *Communication problems.* Check the centre of your house/office. If there is a wall or column here, hang a mirror on it. Keep this area neat and tidy and hang a bronze bell or a metal chime here.

Chapter Three

VAASTU FOR PLOTS

In traditional Vaastu, as practised in centuries gone by, evaluating land was an extensive subject. For today's world, this has been simplified.

While selecting a plot, Vaastu looks at many features — the shape of the plot, plot extensions (if any), which way the plot faces, the slope, the soil conditions, how the plot is aligned to the magnetic axis, and how roads lie in relation to the plot.

The decision regarding a plot of land should not be taken based on any single factor in isolation. A plot should be accepted or rejected keeping in mind the cumulative effect of all the above mentioned factors.

In general, it can be said that the land under consideration should be devoid of rocks and ditches, the soil should be fertile and clean smelling, plants should be plentiful on it, and animals should want to graze on it.

Buying land which is over a graveyard is generally not recommended. In such a situation there are other factors which come into play, like the number of years since it has been in disuse as a graveyard. One must also ascertain whether the negative energies emitted by the dead bodies have been transmuted or neutralised, or if they still exist in discarnate form. The transmutation of energies is a vast subject and out of the purview of this book. If one has a choice, an alternative plot should be considered.

It is important to note that the bifurcation of plots suggested in this chapter to make a plot of an acceptable shape, is only symbolic. You can 'bifurcate' by simply constructing a hedge or a wooden fence, or by tying a copper wire between two poles. However, if major changes are required, the plot should be rectified by a *Vaastu-shilpi* or consultant.

Given here is a traditional prayer, the *Mahamantra*, that is always said during the *puja* held for sanctifying a plot before construction. It is also recommended that a cow with a calf be left to graze on the vacant plot as this neutralizes a lot of negative energies.

Mahamantra

ॐ नमो भगवते वास्तुपुरूषाप महाबलपराक्रमाय
सर्वाधिरासाश्रितशशरीराय ब्रह्मपुत्राय
सकलब्रह्माण्डधारिणे भुभारार्पितमस्तकाय
पुरपतनप्रासादग हवापिसरः कूपादेः
सन्निवेश सान्निध्यकराय सर्वासिद्धिप्रदाय
प्रसन्नबदनाय विश्वंभराय परमपुरूषाय
शक्रवरदाय वास्तोष्पते नमस्ते ॥

ॐ

Aum! I pay obeisance to the all knowing, all powerful, and holy Vaastupurusha, whose presence is the support of all dwellings. Son of Brahma, upholder of the entire creation, on whose head is placed to carry the responsibility of this planet, who is everpresent everywhere in the towns and cities, houses and temples. Bestower of all bounty, of beauty, son of the cosmos, supreme Purusha, granter of boons, Lord of dwellings, obeisance to thee!

Plot shapes that are auspicious

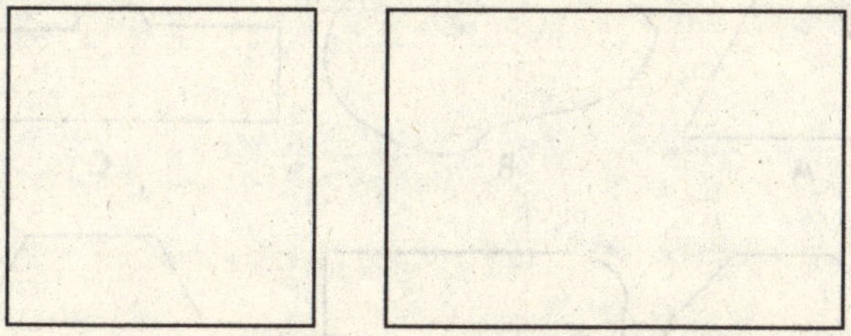

The shape of the plot is a primary consideration. Vaastu considers the square the most perfect, stable, and sacred form. A rectangular plot is auspicious, as is any shape with an even number of sides. However, as discussed earlier, a plot should not be accepted or rejected on one consideration alone. Many aspects, dealt with in this book, should be taken into account before a final decision is made.

Plot shapes that are inauspicious

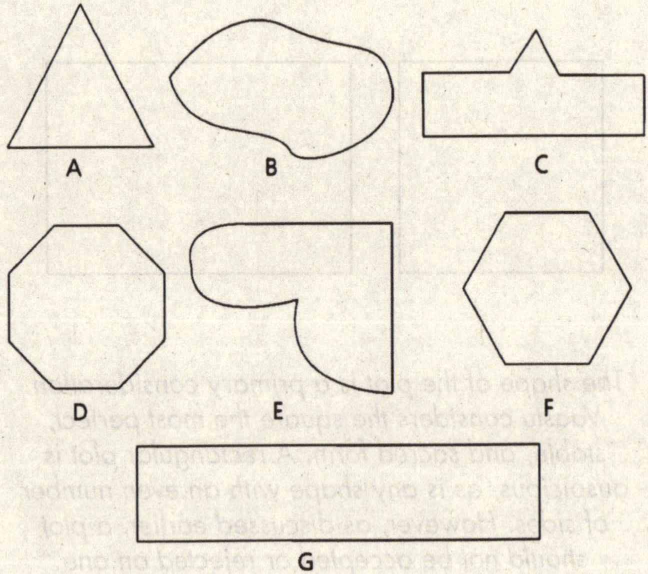

A triangular shaped plot (A), or a plot with three corners is associated with negative energies which bring in problems and are best avoided. Other irregular shapes (B, C, D, E, F) are also not considered beneficial. A thin, long, rectangular plot (G) is also not suitable as it is disproportionate. The correct proportion for a rectangular plot is that the length should be no more than twice the width.

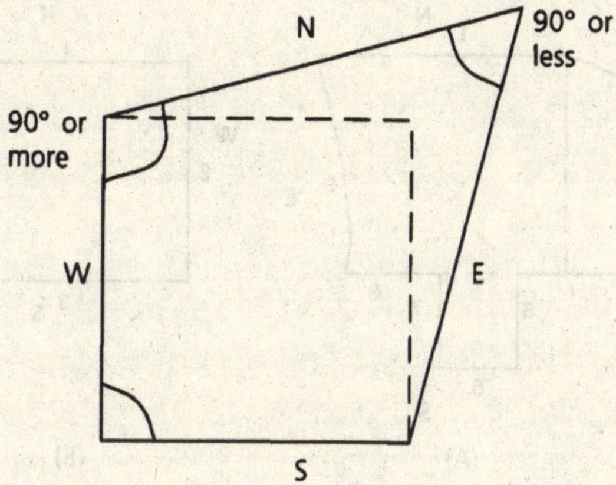

An ideal plot

An ideal shape is square or rectangular, with a little extension towards the north-east.

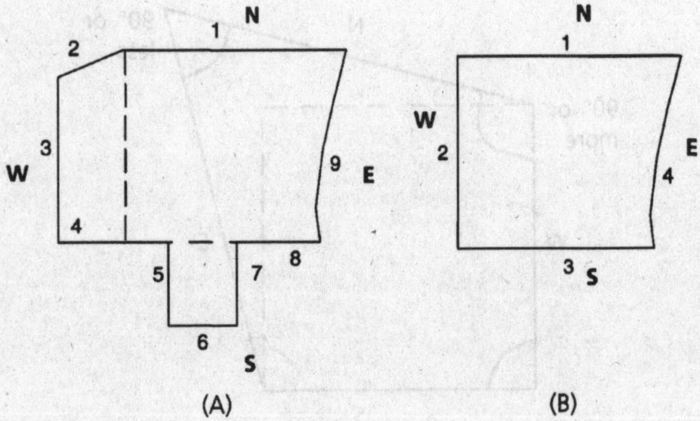

A plot that has been balanced

If a plot of any shape, after rectification, forms a square or a rectangle, then it is balanced. The plot above (A) has 9 sides and is not suitable. To balance it, bifurcate along the dotted lines to get the acceptable shape (B). Note that the bifurcation is only symbolic, so it may be done by a hedge or fence. Copper or silver wires, which have good conductivity, may also be used to bifurcate.

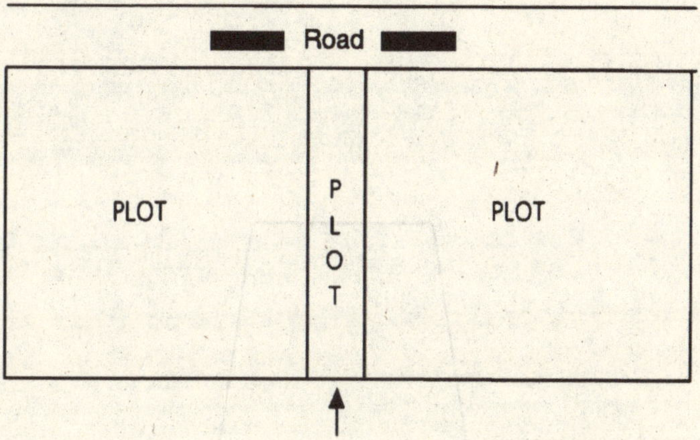

A small plot wedged between big plots

This should be avoided. In general, the auspicious dimensions of a plot are that the length should be, at most, twice the width, i.e. the proportion of length to width should be 2:1. If the length is more than 2:1, it is best avoided as it would be disproportionate. A plot full of rocks, anthills and bones should also be avoided.

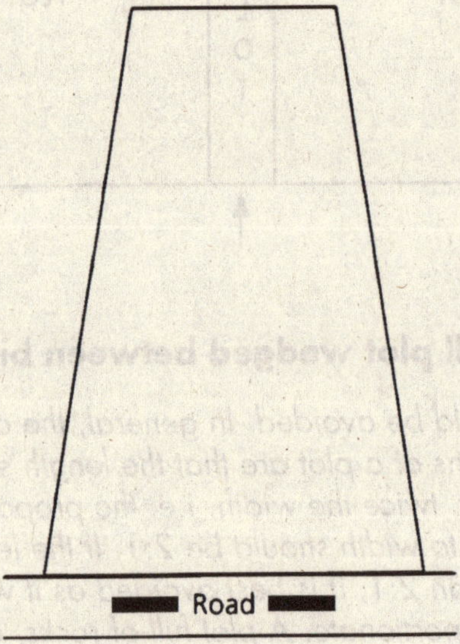

A Sher Mukh (lion-faced) plot

A plot that is wider on the side facing the road than on the opposite side is good for commercial rather than residential use.

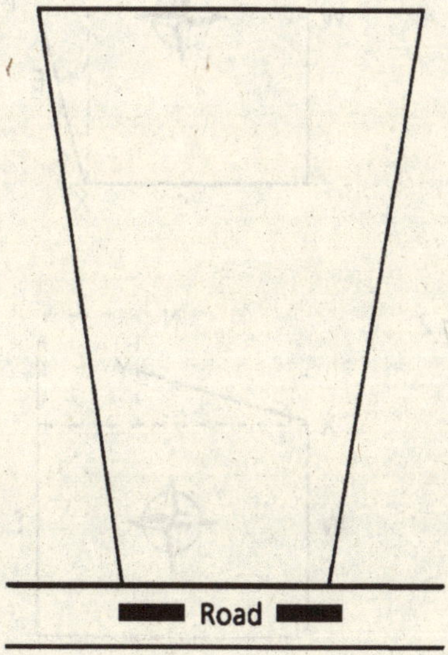

A Gau Mukh (cow-faced) plot

A plot that is narrower on the side facing the road rather than on the opposite side is good for residential, not commerical use.

Plot extensions

Fig. 1

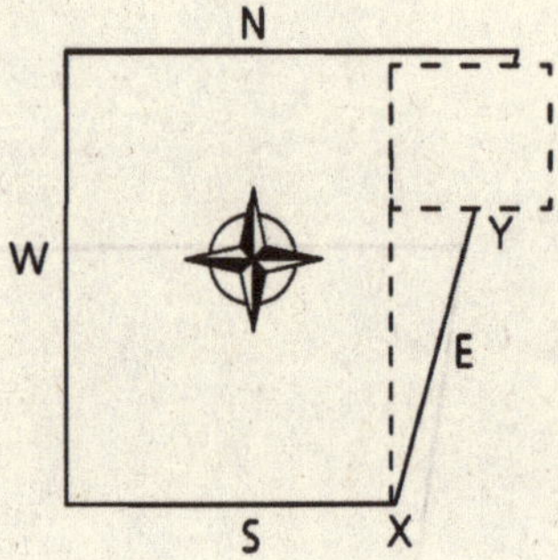

Fig.2

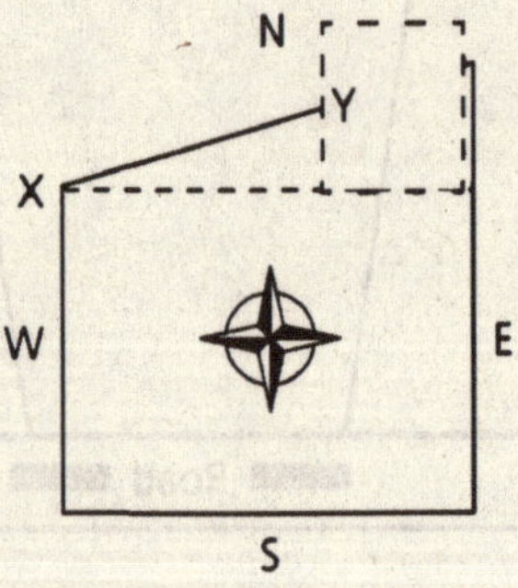

A plot which is extended either east of north-east (Fig. 1) or north of north-east (Fig. 2) is good. Note that such plots are basically L-shaped. However, extensions of a plot may also be along the XY axis as in the diagrams shown here.

Fig.3

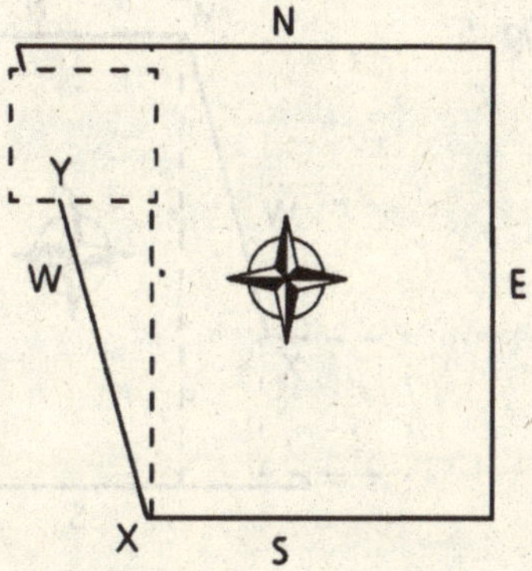

Fig.4

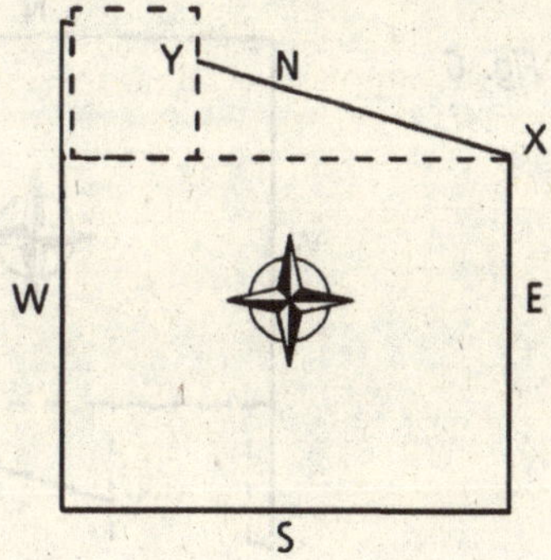

A plot which is extended either west of north-west (Fig. 3) or north of north-west (Fig. 4) is not so good and should be rectified.

Fig. 5

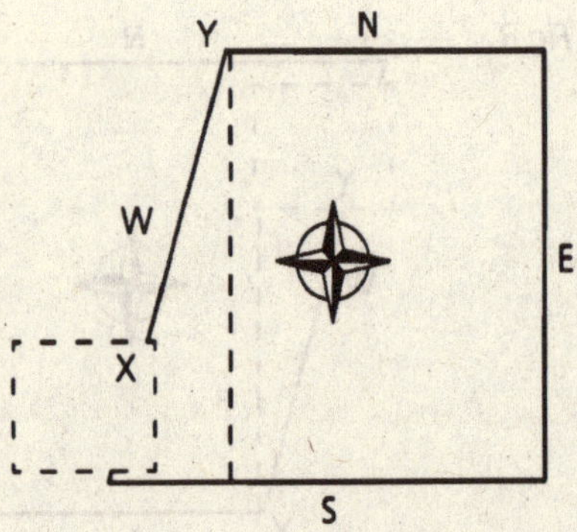

Fig. 6

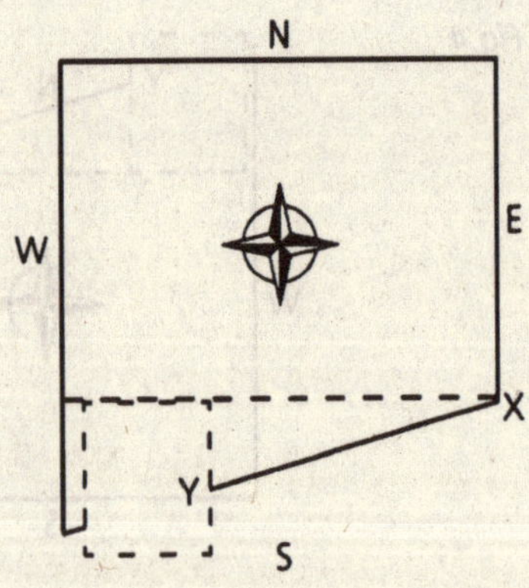

A plot which is extended either west of south-west (Fig. 5) or south of south-west (Fig. 6) is not so good and should be rectified.

Fig. 7

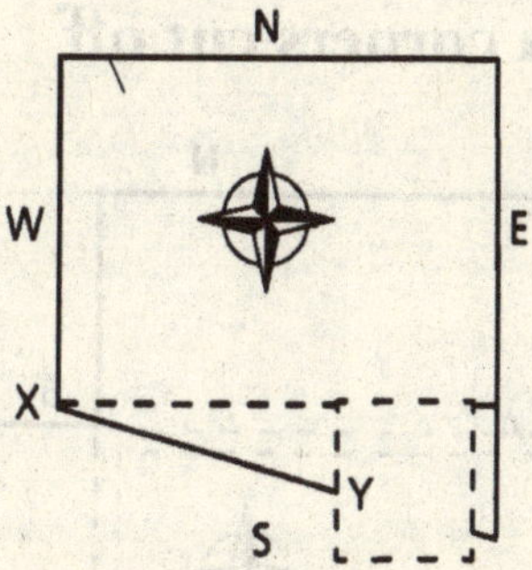

Fig. 8

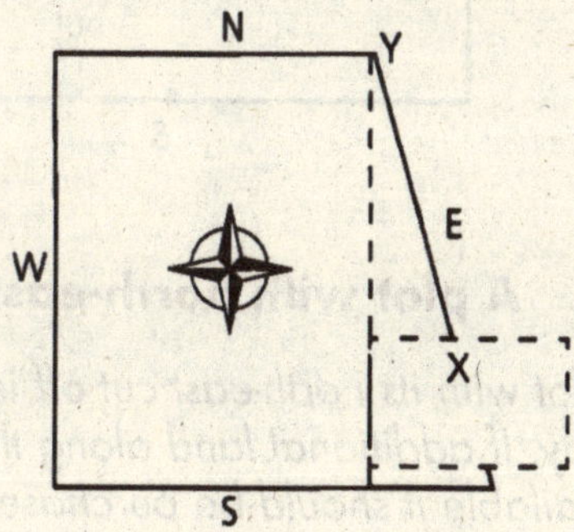

A plot which is extended either south of south-east (Fig. 7) or east of south-east (Fig. 8) is not so good and should be rectified.

Plots with corners cut off

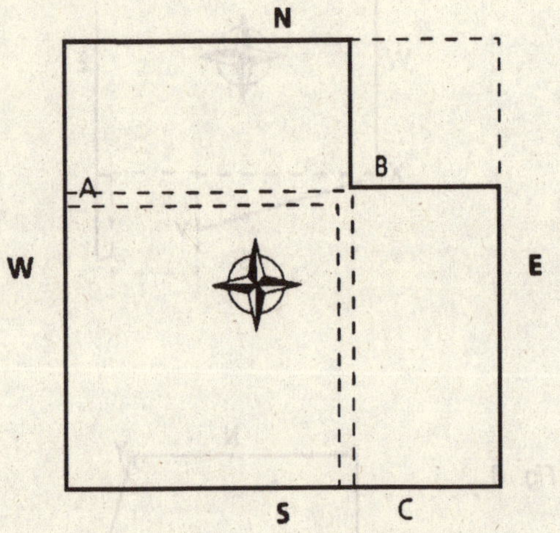

A plot with north-east cut off

A plot with its north-east cut off is like a headless body. If additional land along the dotted line is available it should be purchased immediately. Bifurcating the plot along the double dotted line AB means cutting off the north. Bifurcating the plot along the double dotted line BC means cutting off the east. Neither is auspicious.

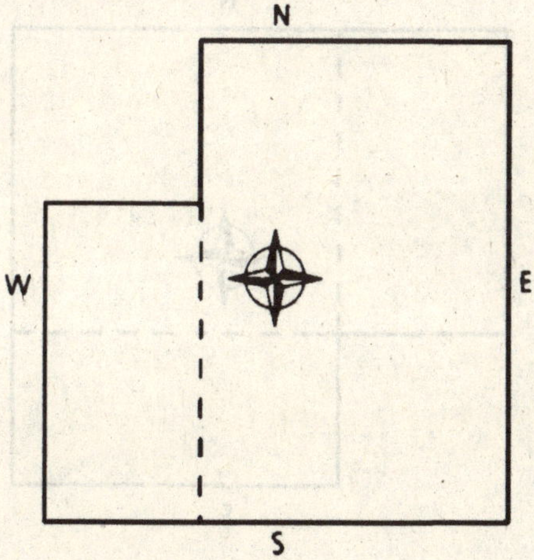

A plot with north-west cut off

A plot with its north-west cut off is not good. It can be rectified by bifurcation along the dotted line.

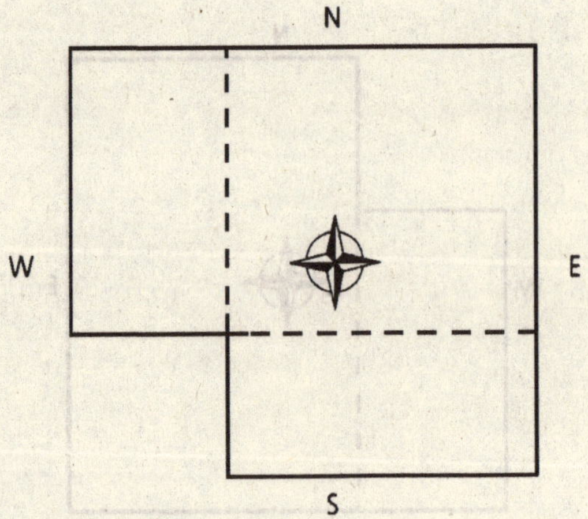

A plot with south-west cut off

A plot with its south-west cut off is not good. It can be rectified by bifurcation along the dotted line on the south or west boundary.

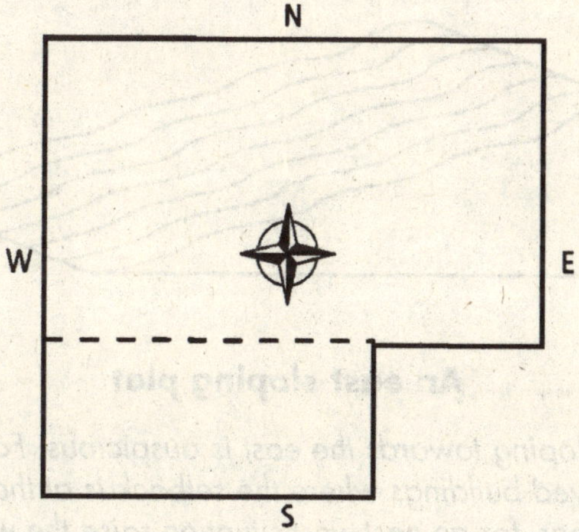

A plot with south-east cut off

If the south-east is cut off, the defect can be removed by bifurcating along the dotted line.

The Slope

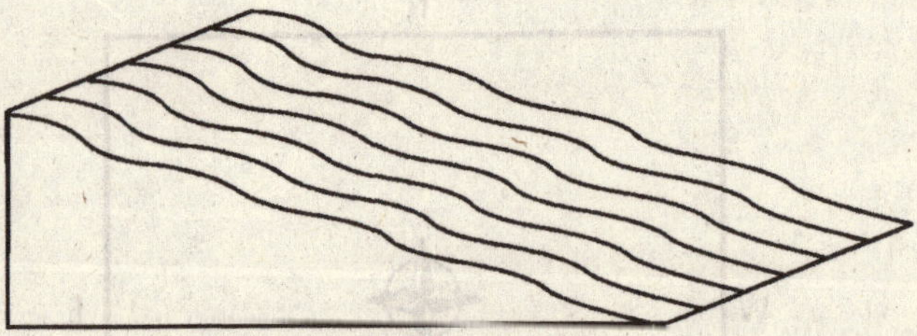

An east-sloping plot

Land sloping towards the east is auspicious. For multi-storeyed buildings where the setback is at the front and rear, for an east-west situation raise the western side and have a slope towards east.

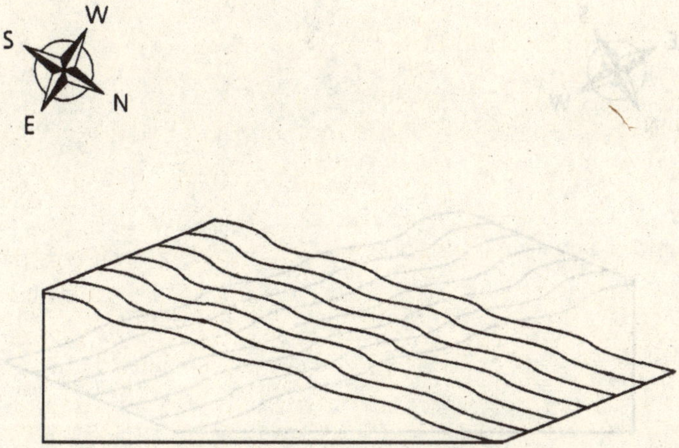

A north-sloping plot

Land sloping towards the north is also considered very good. For a multi-storeyed building where the setback is the same at the front and rear, for a north-south situation raise the southern slope and have a slope towards north.

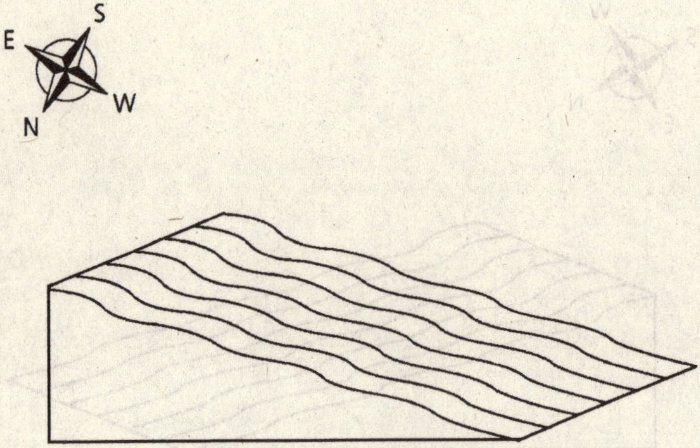

A west-sloping plot

Land sloping towards the west is not considered good. But if the soil smells nice, earth can be dug out from the eastern/northern corner and filled in towards the west, thereby making the land slope towards the north or east.

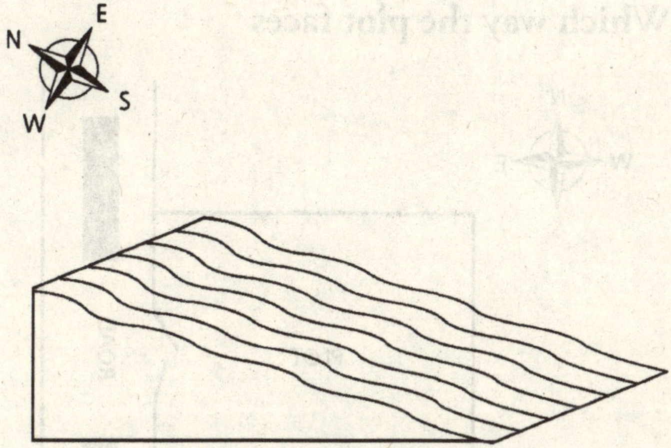

A south-sloping plot

Land sloping towards the south is also not considered good. But if the same exercise as suggested for west-sloping plot can be carried out to make the land slope eastward or northward, the unwanted energies can be negated.

Which way the plot faces

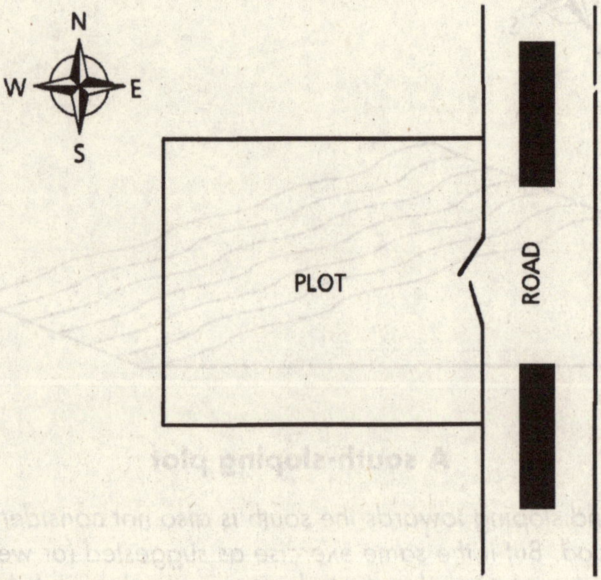

An east-facing plot

An east-facing plot is considered very auspicious because it receives a lot of solar energy. According to Vaastu, the north and east hold a special significance as solar energy comes from the east, and the earth's magnetic axis runs north-south. The north-east is thus a conjunction of solar and magnetic energy.

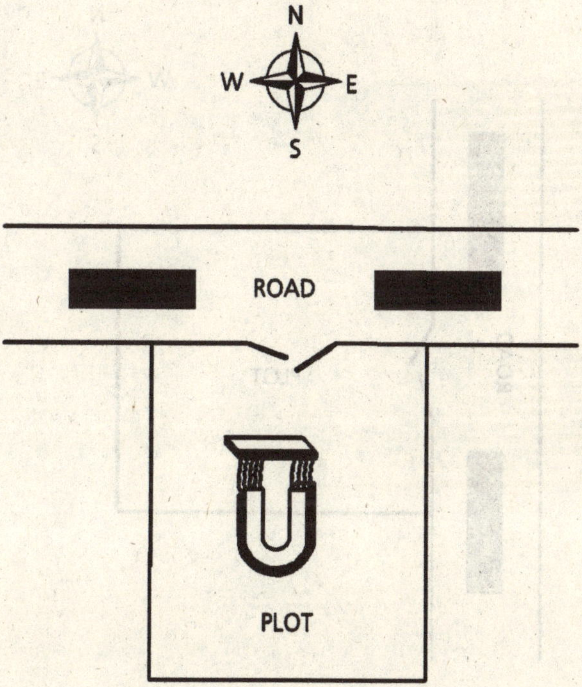

A north-facing plot

A north-facing plot is also good as it is on the magnetic axis and invites magnetic energy.

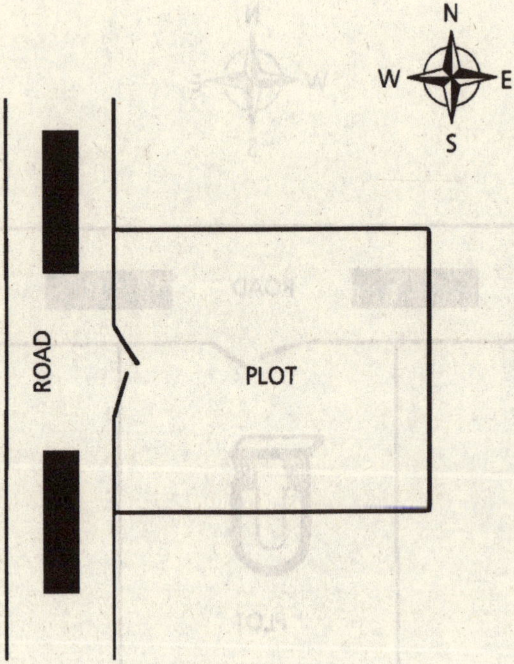

A west-facing plot

A west-facing plot is average for residential purposes. However, it is good for businessmen, specially for the entertainment business such as cinemas, clubs and pubs.

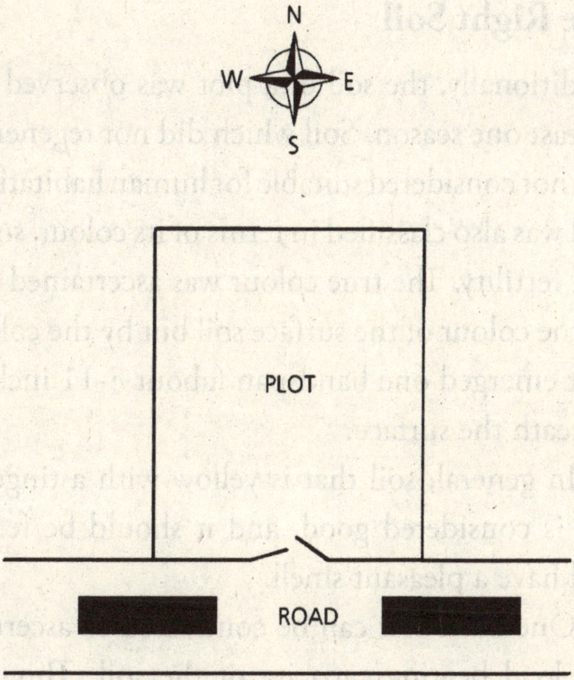

A south-facing plot

A south-facing plot is average for residential purposes but auspicious for people in the food business.

The Right Soil

Traditionally, the soil of a plot was observed for at least one season. Soil which did not regenerate was not considered suitable for human habitation. Soil was also classified in terms of its colour, smell and fertility. The true colour was ascertained not by the colour of the surface soil but by the colour that emerged one handspan (about 8-11 inches) beneath the surface.

In general, soil that is yellow with a tinge of red is considered good, and it should be fertile and have a pleasant smell.

One basic test can be conducted to ascertain the load bearing capacity of the soil. This will define the kind of foundation that must be used. Dig a pit 3 cubic feet in volume (see below) at the centre of the plot, and fill it back with the same earth that was dug out.

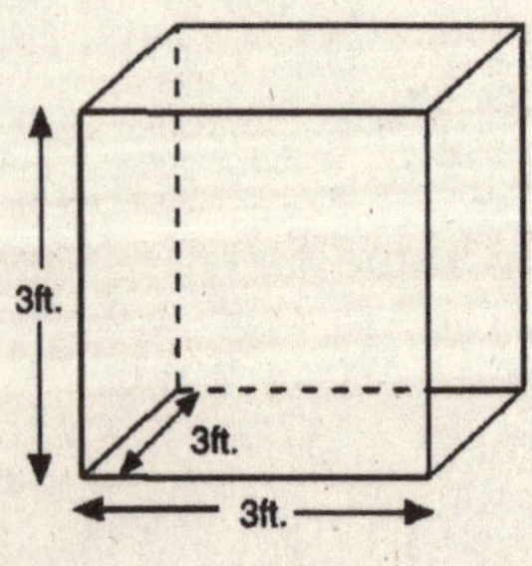

If the re-filled ground is level at the top, the soil is average.

If the re-filled ground results in a mound formation, the plot is very good.

If the level is depressed after re-filling the earth, it indicates the presence of negative energies and the place should preferably be left alone.

If the plot is raised or depressed at the centre, it is not auspicious. Depending upon the soil and other environmental factors, it can be balanced by levelling or filling the centre. The earth dug out (in case of elevation) should be dumped towards the south-west boundary wall.

Similarly, if the plot of land is raised towards the east or north, the mound should be removed and dumped along the west or south boundary wall.

At the same time, a plot of land raised towards the south or west is considered very good.

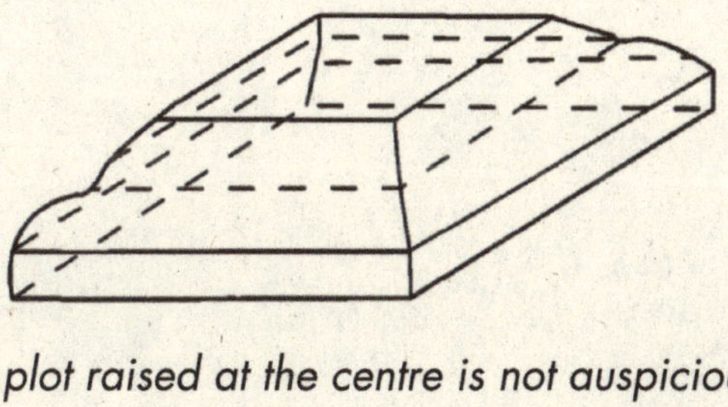

A plot raised at the centre is not auspicious

The magnetic axis

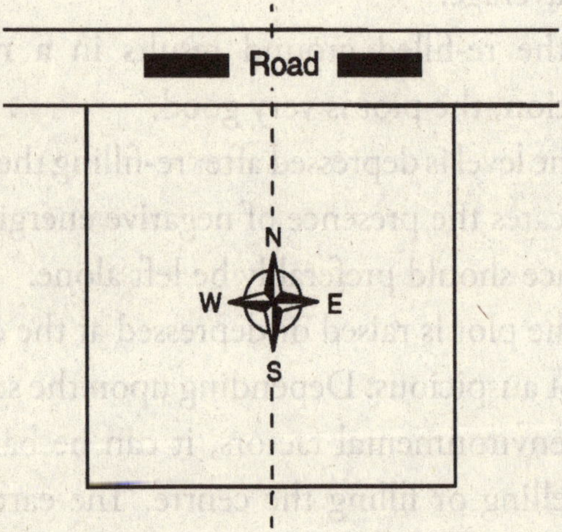

Plot aligned with the magnetic axis

For an explanation of the magnetic axis see pg. 13. A plot that has a north-south axis, i.e. aligned to the magnetic axis (the dotted line along north-south) is auspicious.

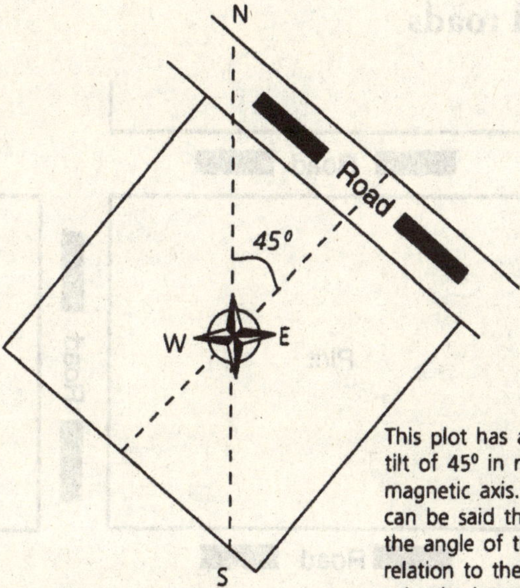

This plot has an angle or tilt of 45° in relation to the magnetic axis. In general, it can be said that the lesser the angle of the plot in relation to the magnetic axis, the better.

Plot at an angle to the magnetic axis

A plot which is at an angle with the magnetic axis (dotted line NS) can still be balanced, if we view factors such as the side it is facing and what objects exist in the vicinity. The following are good — an electrical transformer in the south-east, a high rise building at SW, a play school (symbolising movement) at NW, or a temple at NE. Note that these should not touch the actual boundary of the plot.

Plots and roads

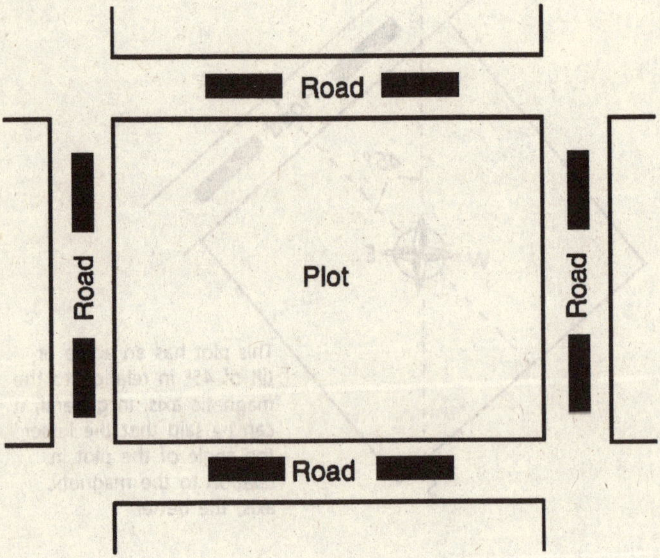

Roads on all four sides

A plot with roads running on all four sides that are not spearing roads is good for commercial and residential purposes because energy flows uniformly on all sides.

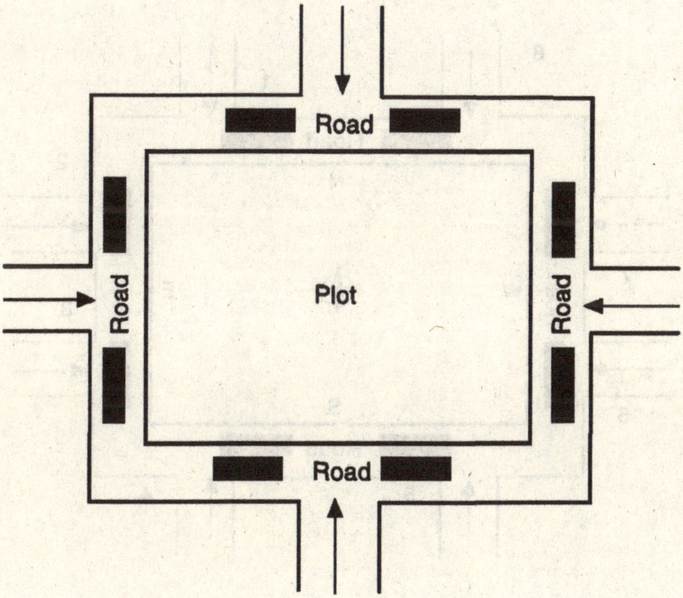

Spearing roads on all four sides

When there are roads on all four sides but they are spearing roads, it is not auspicious.

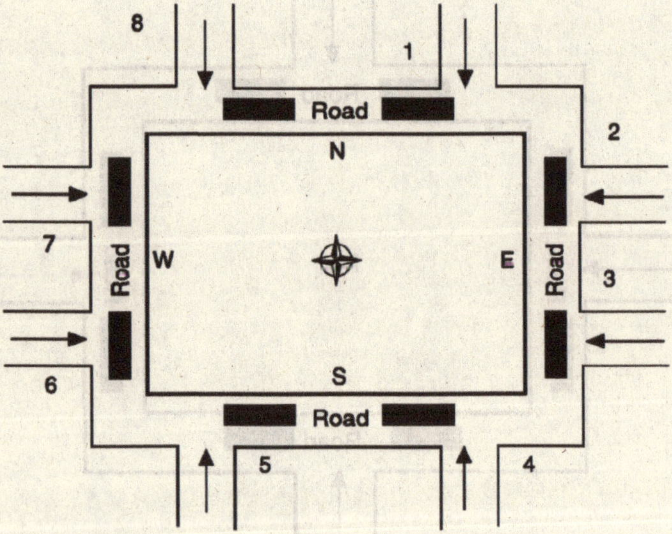

Numerous spearing roads

Spearing roads at 1, 2, 4 and 7 are good but not at 3, 5, 6 and 8.

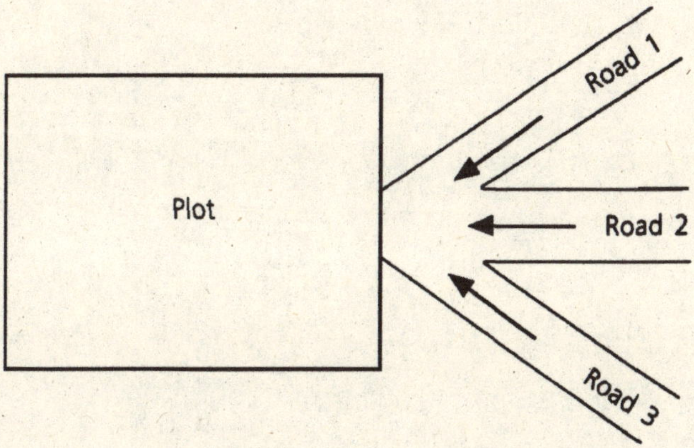

A spearing road on one side

A plot with one spearing road such as Road 1, Road 2 or Road 3 is not good at all.

Chapter Four

EVALUATE YOUR PLOT

Caution

The reader is cautioned not to draw any hasty conclusions because of the positive or negative score obtained in any Evaluation Exercise in this book.

Such scores are not to be considered in isolation. In some cases, the high or low score may not hold good at all, because of the influence of other factors. A conclusion should only be drawn after considering the overall view.

None of the Score Sheets are meant to scare the reader. The exercises are aimed at informing the reader and making him aware of the various facets of Vaastu.

How to do the Evaluation Exercises

1. Note that you will require a magnetic compass for Exercises 1, 2, 3, 4, 5, 7, 9.
2. Use a protractor (shown below) to measure an angle for Exercise 8.

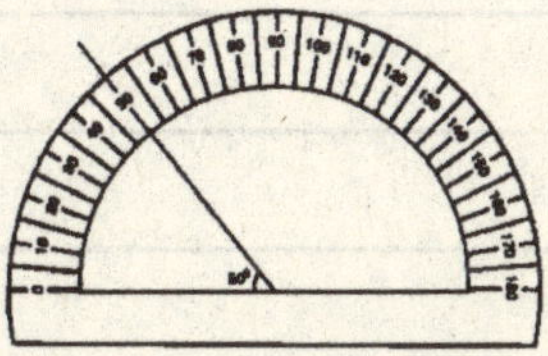

3. Start with Exercise 1 (pg. 60). Use a compass to ascertain which side your plot faces. If for example, it faces north, you score 8 points. Circle 8 in Exercise 1.
4. Now turn to the Final Score Sheet on pg. 69. Put 8 in the column Your Score for Question no. 1.
5. Do the same for Exercises 2-9.
6. Add your total score in the Final Score Sheet (pg. 69) and write it in the Total column. The total points indicate how favourable your plot is.
7. Check your score on the Rating Scale (pg. 70).

Exercise 1

Which side does the plot face?

(See pages 44 to 47)

Direction	Points
East	10
North-east	9
North	8
North-west	7
South-east	6
West	5
South	4
South-west	3

Exercise 2

Where are the spearing roads?

(See pages 54 to 56)

Direction	Points
East of north-east	10
North of north-east	9
West of north-west	8
South of south-east	7
East of south-east	6
North of north-west	5
West of south-west	4
South and south-west	3

Exercise 3

Which direction does the plot slope towards?

(See pages 40 to 43)

Direction	Points
North-east	10
East	9
North	8
North-west	7
South-east	6
South	5
West	4
South-west	3

Exercise 4

In which direction is the plot raised?

(See pages 40 to 43)

Direction	Points
South-west	10
West	9
South	8
South-east	7
North-west	6
North	5
East	4
North-east	3

Exercise 5

What is the shape of the plot?

(See pages 25 to 31)

Shape	Points
Square with north-east extended	10
Square	9
Rectangular	8
Hexagonal or 6-sided	7
Octagonal or 8-sided	6
Circular / oval	5
Any other shape which can be rectified	4
Triangular or any shape which cannot be rectified	3

Exercise 6

What is the quality of the soil?

(See pages 48 to 49)

Qualities	Points
Yellowish red with pleasant smell	10
Reddish with pleasant smell	9
Yellowish with pleasant smell	8
Rocky with good surroundings	7
Sandy with good surroundings	6
Sandy with unpleasant odour	5
Rocky with unpleasant odour	4
Black and marshy soil	3

Exercise 7

Are there any plot extensions?

(See pages 32 to 39)

Type	Points
Square or rectangle with extension at north-east	10
Any shape having even number of sides with extension at north-east	9
Any shape having odd number of sides with extension at north-east	8
Extension at south-east *(Good for women)*	7
Extension at north-west *(Good for women)*	6
Extension at west	5
Extension at south	4
Extension at south-west	3

Exercise 8

What is the angle of tilt in relation to the magnetic axis?

(See pages 51 to 52)

Angle	Points
0–5°	10
5–10°	9
10–15°	8
15–20°	7
20–25°	6
25–30°	5
30–35°	4
35–45°	3

Exercise 9

What are the surroundings?

Surroundings	Points
A lake or a water body towards north-east	20
A lake or a water body at east	18
A lake or a water body at north	16
Electric sub-station at south-east	14
Electric sub-station at north-west	12
A hillock in the south-west	10
A hillock in the south	8
A hillock in the west	6

Final Score Sheet for Plot Evaluation

Exercises	Points	Your Score
1. Which side does the plot face?	10	
2. Where are the spearing roads?	10	
3. Which side is the plot sloping towards?	10	
4. Where is the plot raised?	10	
5. What is the shape of the plot?	10	
6. What is the quality of the soil?	10	
7. Are there any plot extensions?	10	
8. What is the angle of the tilt with respect to the magnetic axis of the earth?	10	
9. What are the surroundings?	20	
Total	100	

Rating Scale

Score	Interpretation
100	Excellent
80-99	Very good
51-79	Good
upto 50	Average

Chapter Five

VAASTU FOR HOMES

Our home is a sacred space, a centre point in our lives and the place where we replenish our energies. A Vaastu oriented home means it will be a tranquil place, harnessing all the positive forces of nature. It will be clean, uncluttered, well lit, well ventilated, with a good flow of energy moving through it, which will draw towards it good fortune and positive energies.

Ideally, the major part of the house should be in the south-west quadrant, leaving more space to the north and east as compared to the south and west. For large sized plots such as farm houses, large spaces can be left open to the north and east.

Keep in mind that the main entrance of the house is a most powerful feature, deeply connected to the well-being of the family. Traditionally, the *dwara* (or door) has been treated with great sanctity as through it one enters the inner domain of family life. It should be well proportioned, strong, with no creaking sounds. It should be adorned with plants and auspicious images. No shadow should fall on the entrance, nor should there be a wall immediately in front of it. There should not be a litter or garbage bin outside it either. In fact, the entrance should reflect the order and harmony of the inner spaces of the house.

Ideal location of a house/flat on a plot

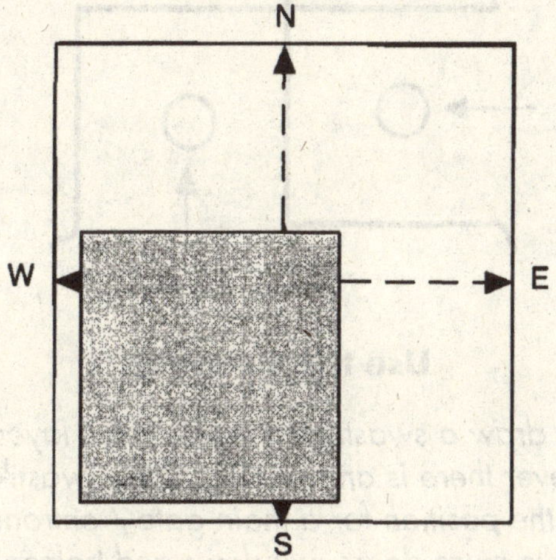

Position of a house on a plot

Leave more open space in the east and north as compared to the south and west. Construct in the south-west quadrant.

Position of the main door

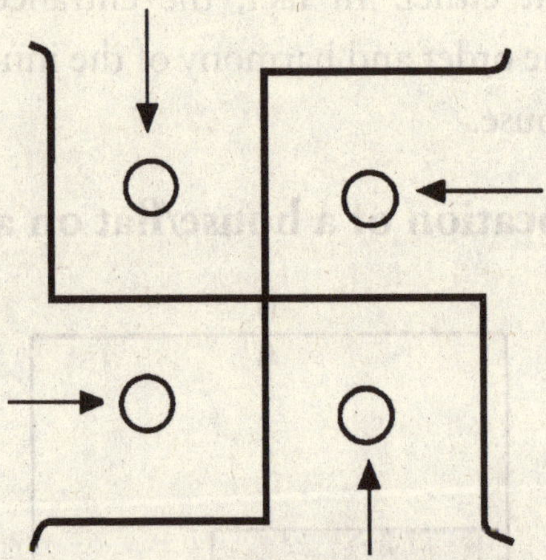

Use the swastika

Simply draw a swastika symbol on the layout plan. Wherever there is an opening in the swastika, that can be the position for a main gate / entrance door. Also, have more doors, windows and balconies in the east and north as compared to the south and west. Placing the main door in the north-east is best.

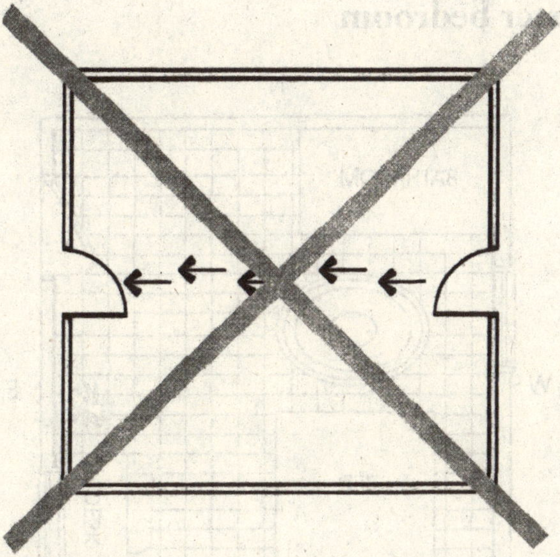

Do not have the entrance and the exit doors in a straight line as then whatever comes in tends to flow out. Also, do not place doors at the precise centre of a cardinal point, as this position is generally used in temples.

Master bedroom

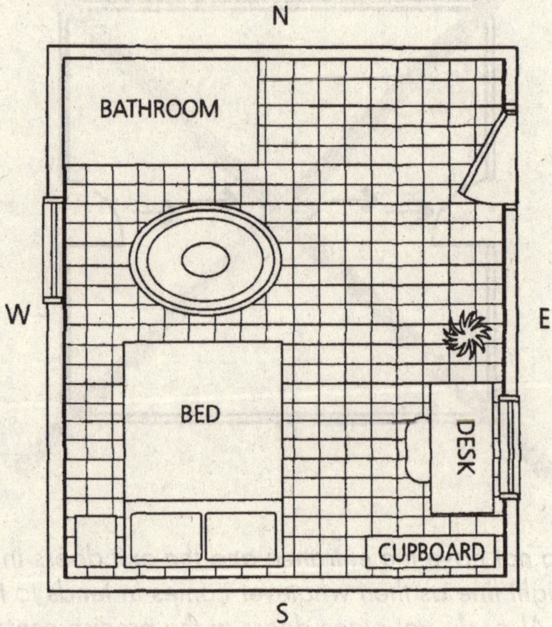

Location of master bedroom

The master bedroom should be in the south-west quadrant, preferably the corner. The floor level should ideally be 6" above the rest of the house. The north-west quadrant is the only other alternative. Avoid other quadrants.

While sitting at the desk you should face east. The bathroom should be in the north-west corner of the bedroom.

For a balcony in the south-west have lots of plants; do not leave the space vacant. A south-west balcony should be protected from harmful ultra-violet rays, specially in the afternoon.

The position in which you sleep is important. It is advisable to sleep with your head towards the south. Sleeping with the head towards the east is also acceptable. However, do not sleep with your head towards the north. The head of a body is the north, and, since similar magnetic poles repel each other, the electro-magnetic waves in your body will get disrupted and lead to poor sleep and ill-health.

Drawing and dining rooms

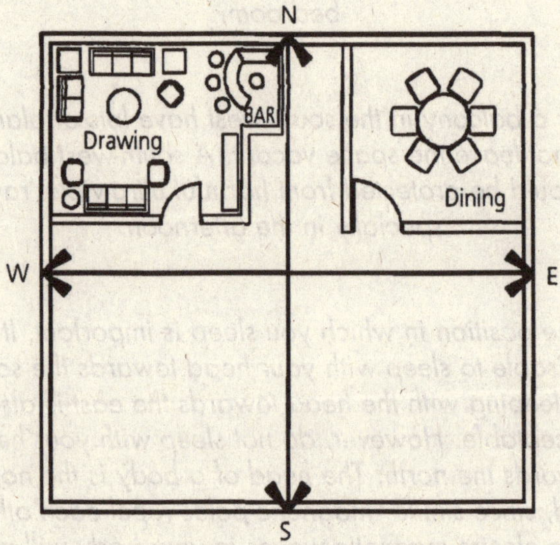

Location of drawing and dining rooms

It is advisable to have the drawing and dining rooms along the east or north wall. The dining room should be more towards the north-east and preferably be placed close to the kitchen. Note that heaters and fireplaces should be at the south-east. Plants are auspicious anywhere.

Children's bedroom

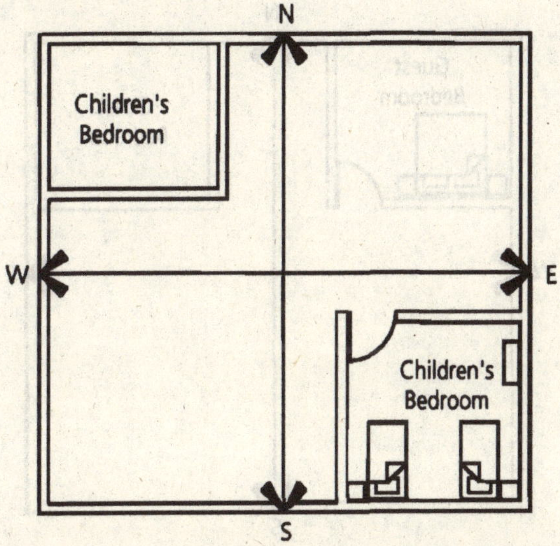

Location of the children's bedroom

The north-west and the south-east is very auspicious. The south-west is to be avoided. The north-east corner can also be considered. Since east denotes enlightenment, it is suggested that children study facing the east.

Guest room

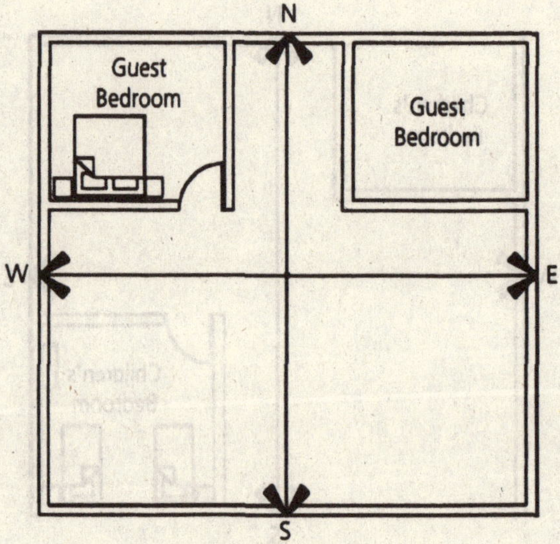

Location of the guest room

The north-west corner or quadrant is ideal for the guest room. This quadrant is the centre for Vayu or wind and denotes movement. Guests placed here means that they will not stay too long. Otherwise build the guest room in the north-east quadrant.

Puja room

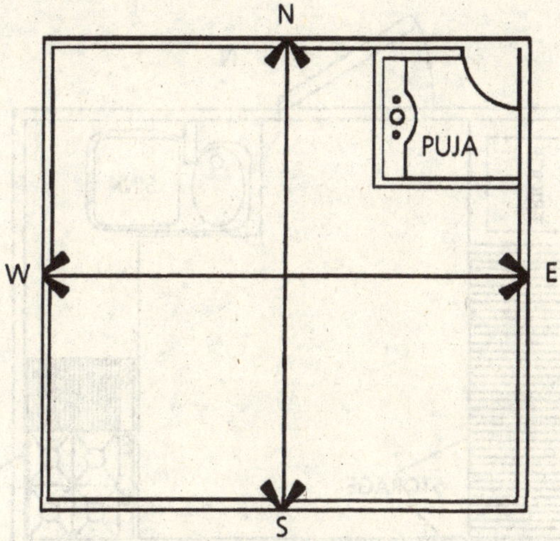

Location of the puja room

Deep devotion is best rooted in the heart. However, if you wish to have a puja room it should ideally be in the north-east. The deities can be facing east, west or north. If they happen to be facing the south, it is suggested that an idol of Lord Shiva or Hanumanji be kept.

Kitchen

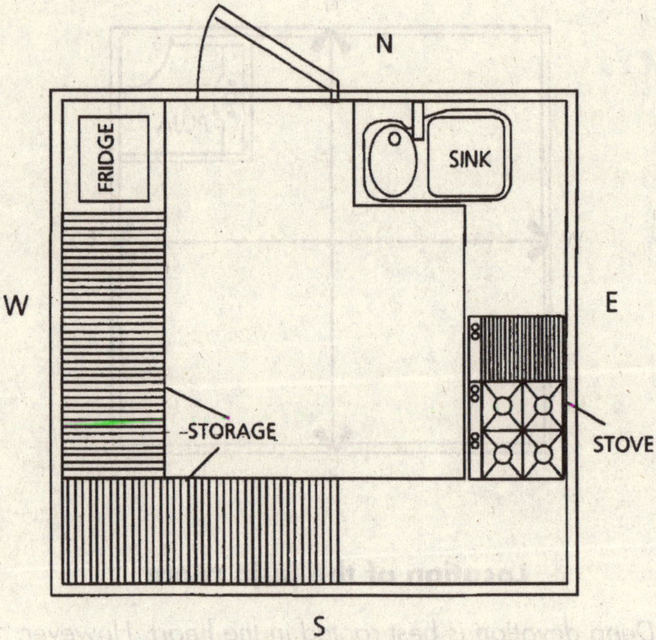

Ideal location of Kitchen

- *The ideal place for a kitchen is the south-east quadrant, which is the quadrant for fire. The other possibility is the north-west which is the quadrant for air. It is appropriate because air supports fire.*

- *Have the sink/wash-basin along the north or north-east.*

- *Do your cooking facing the east or the north and do not have your back to a door while you cook.*
- *Keep your fridge in the north-west corner.*
- *Store your rations along the south-west wall.*
- *Note that the stove should not be placed directly opposite a door.*
- *Something orange in colour (symbolic of fire) should be in the kitchen.*

Staircase

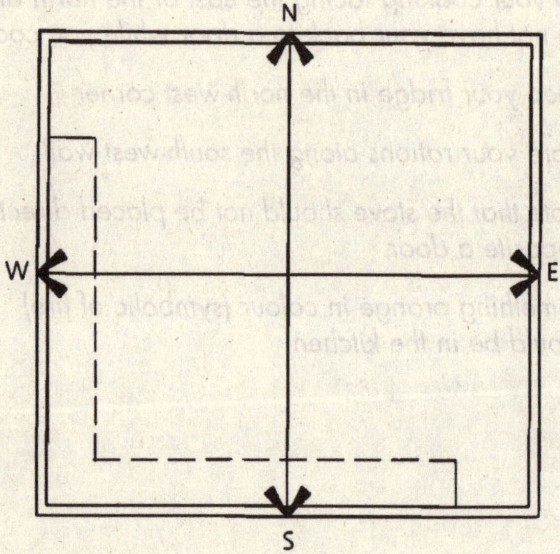

Position of staircase

If there is a staircase, it should preferably be along the south-west wall.

Under the staircase

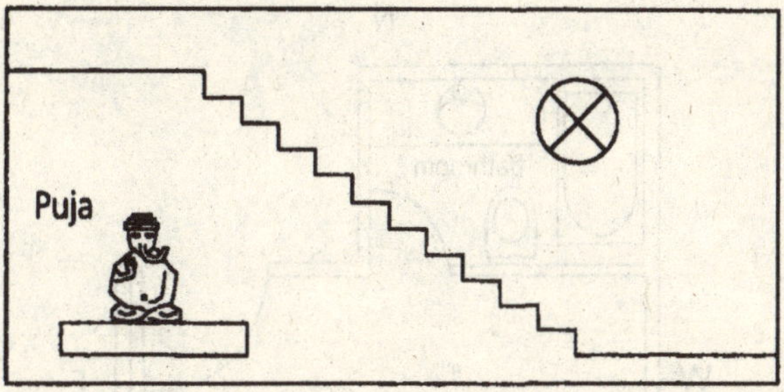

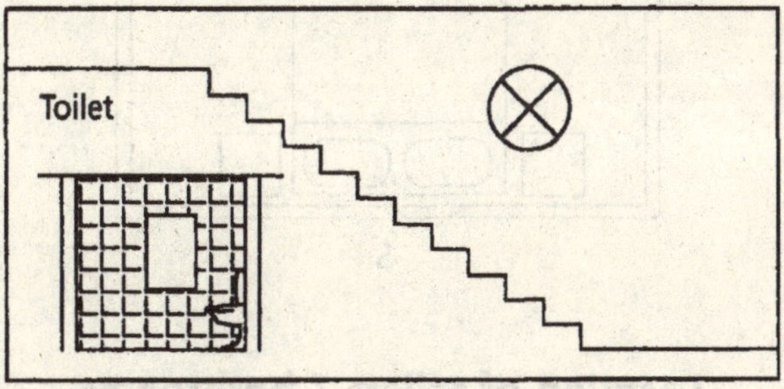

Do not have a puja room or toilet under the staircase.

Toilets/bathrooms

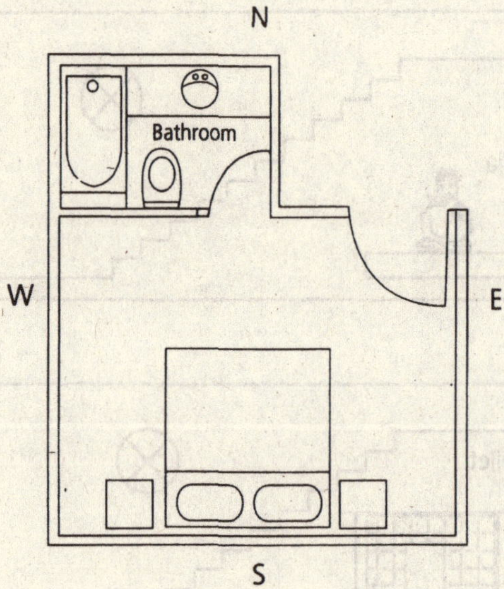

Location of toilets / bathrooms

Today's homes have them together, in the same area, so they should be towards the north-west corner of the bedroom. If they are separate, then the bathroom can even be towards the east or north and the w.c. towards the west, or alternatively, the south. However, the w.c. should never be in the north-east or south-west corners.

Mezzanine

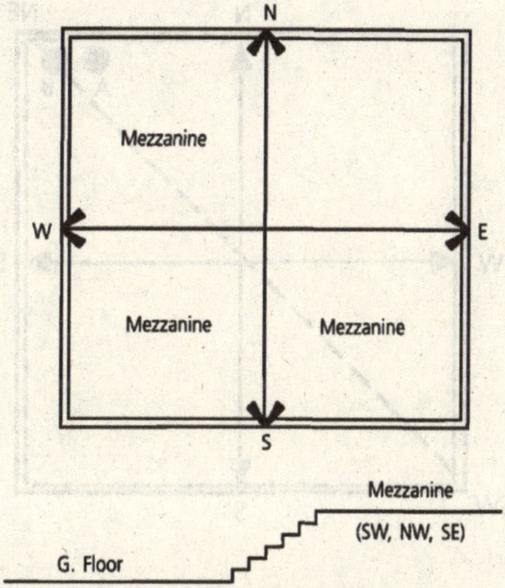

Location of mezzanine

Construct this ideally in the south-west quadrant, alternatively in the south-east or the north-west. Avoid the north-east.

Tubewell/underground tank

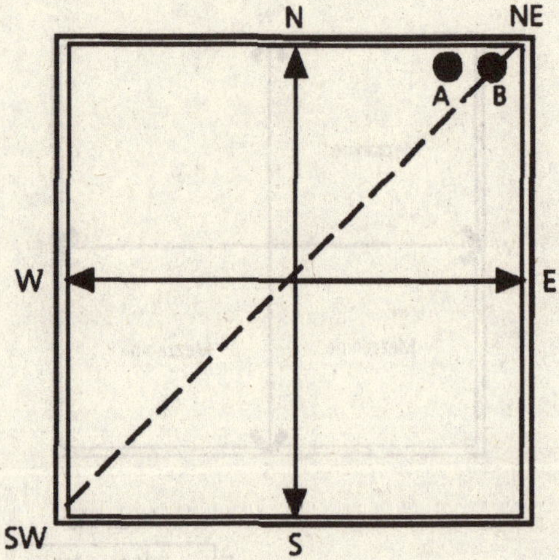

Location of tubewell/underground tank

Let the tubewell or underground tank be in the north-east quadrant (as in A), avoiding the diagonal between the north-east and south-west (as in B). While designing a building it is important to remember that the sewage pipes should be placed at a point farthest from the water source, and can be on any side.

Overhead tank

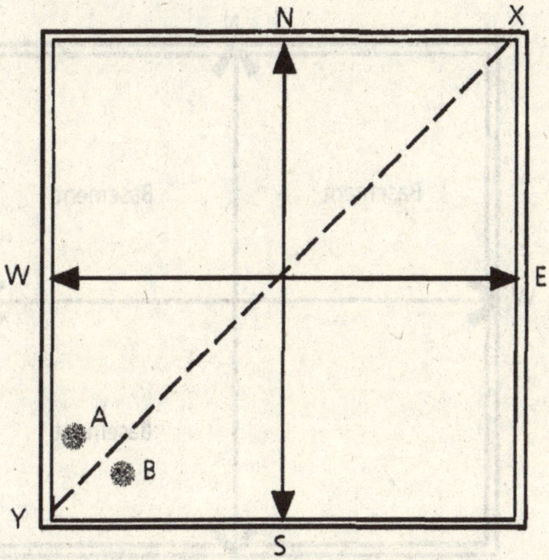

Location of the overhead tank

Let the overhead tank be in the south-west quadrant either A or B avoiding the diagonal XY.

Basement

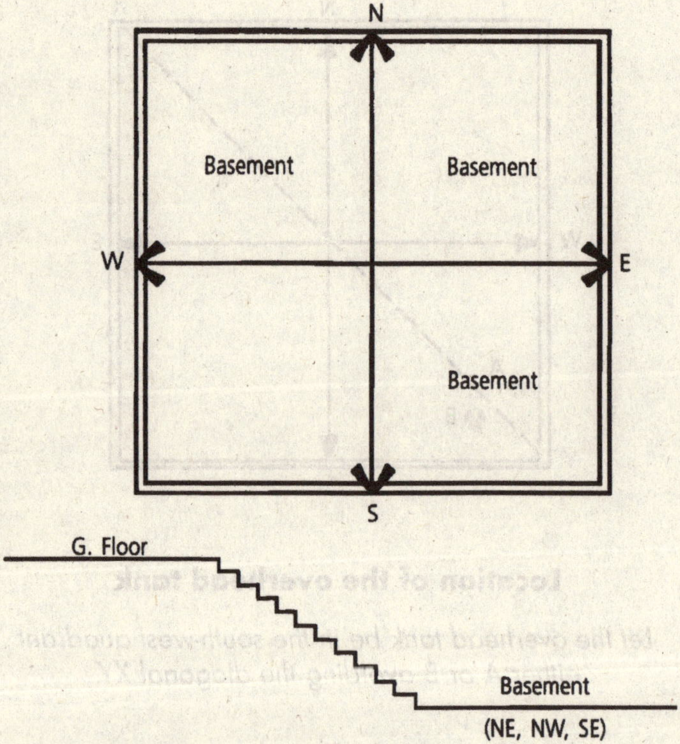

Location of the basement

The north-east quadrant is ideal. Alternatively, either the north-west or the south-east. Avoid the south-west.

Garage

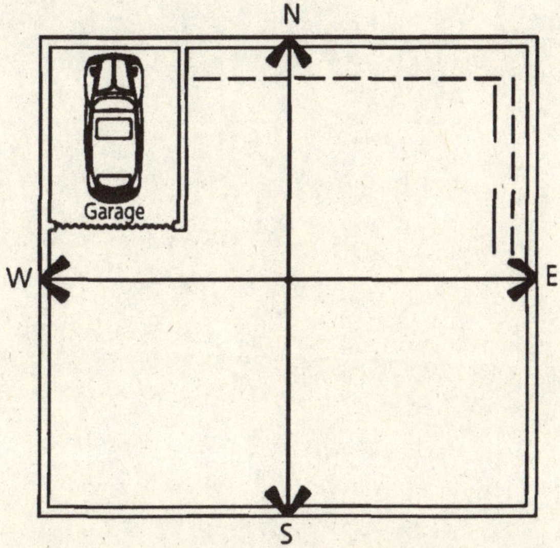

Location of the garage

Build the garage preferably in the north-west, or otherwise anywhere along the dotted line. Park your car facing the north or east.

Chapter Six

EVALUATE YOUR HOME

How to do the Evaluation Exercises

1. Note that you will need a magnetic compass to do these exercises.
2. Start with Exercise 1 (pg. 95). See where your main entrance is positioned. If, for example, it is placed at east, you score 9 points. Circle number 9 in Exercise 1.
3. Now turn to the Final Score Sheet on pg. 105. Put 9 in the column Your Score for Qucstion 1.
4. Do the same for Exercises 2-10.
5. Add all your scores in the Final Score Sheet (pg. 105) and write it in the Total column. The total points indicate how favourable your house or flat is.
6. Check your score on the Rating Scale (pg. 106).

Exercise 1

Position of the main door/gate

(See pages 74 to 75)

Direction	**Points**
North-east	10
East	9
North	8
North-west	7
South-east	6
West	5
South	4
South-west	3

Exercise 2

Position of the kitchen

(*See pages 82-83*)

Direction	Points
South-east	10
North-west	9
East	8
West	7
South	6
North	5
North-east	4
South-west	3

Exercise 3

Position of the master bedroom

(See pages 76-77)

Direction	Points
South-west	10
South	9
West	8
North-west	7
North	6
East	5
South-east	4
North-east	3

Exercise 4

Position of the children's bedroom

(See page 79)

Direction	Points
North-west	10
South-east	9
North	8
East	7
North-east	6
West	5
South	4
South-west	3

Exercise 5

Position of the guest room

(See page 80)

Direction	**Points**
North-west	10
North	9
East	8
North-east	7
South-east	6
West	5
South	4
South-west	3

Exercise 6

Position of the drawing/dining rooms

(See page 78)

Direction	**Points**
East	10
North	9
North-east	8
South-east	7
North-west	6
West	5
South	4
South-west	3

Exercise 7

Position of tube-well/underground tank.

(See page 88)

Direction	Points
North-east	10
East	9
North	8
North-west	7
West	6
South	5
South-east	4
South-west/Centre	3

Exercise 8

Position of the toilet/bathrooms

(See page 86)

Direction	Points
North-west	10
West	9
South	8
North	7
East	6
South-east	5
South-west	4
North-east	3

Exercise 9

Position of garage/servants' quarters

(See page 91)

Direction	Points
North-west	10
North	9
East	8
North-east	7
South-east	6
West	5
South	4
South-west	3

Exercise 10

Position of the house on the plot

(See page 73)

Position of the house	**Points**
House on the south-west of plot	10
House on the south of plot	9
House on the west of plot	8
House on the north-west of plot	7
House on the south-east of plot	6
House on the north of plot	5
House on the east of plot	4
House on the north-east of plot	3

Final Score Sheet for houses and flats

Exercises	Points	Your Score
1. Position of main door/ gate	10	
2. Position of the kitchen	10	
3. Position of master bedroom	10	
4. Position of children's bedroom	10	
5. Position of guest room	10	
6. Position of drawing/ dining room	10	
7. Position of tubewell/tank	10	
8. Position of toilets/ bathrooms	10	
9. Position of garage/ servants' room	10	
10. Position of house on plot	10	
Total	100	

Rating Scale

Score	Interpretation
100	Excellent
80-99	Very good
51-79	Good
upto 50	Average

Chapter Seven

VAASTU FOR SHOPS AND OFFICES

The work space is no less sacred than the home. Indeed, in view of the fact that the energies of many people congregate at one place, it requires even more careful planning than a home.

Since the office is an area of high activity the energy flow and movement should be harmonious. Factors such as ample natural light, good ventilation, uncluttered work spaces (especially at the centre), plenty of plants, and the presence of a water body are some elements that would be appropriate.

Special attention should be paid to the location of the shop/office, placement of the work stations, doors, and ventilators, position of the stocks and cash box, electrical equipment, heavy machinery, and the puja room. Remember, a harmonious working environment means prosperity for all.

Location of shops/offices

Fig. 1

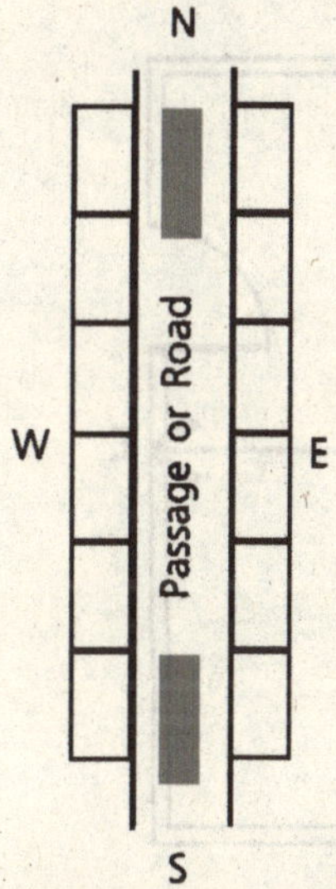

Fig. 2

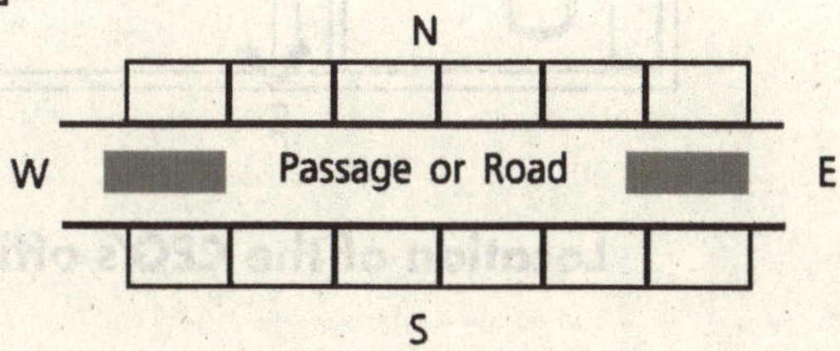

Facing rows of shops/offices

Fig. 1 shows a road going north-south and a row of shops/offices on each side of the road, facing each other. Fig. 2 shows a similar situation, but here the road goes east-west. Both are acceptable.

Head of operations

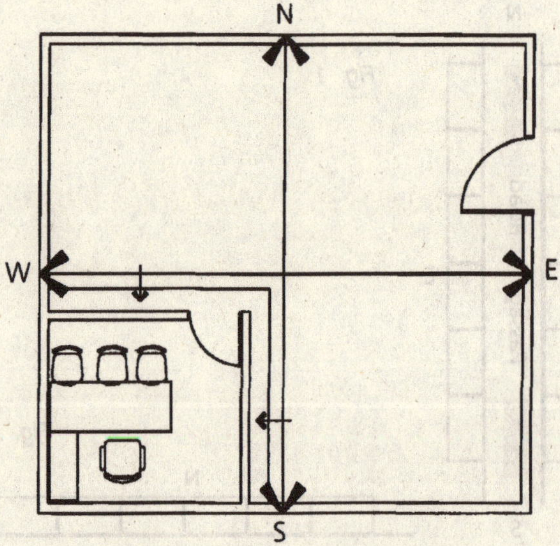

Location of the CEO's office

The offices of Director or CEO should be along the south-west wall and raised 6 inches higher than the office floor.

Sales and marketing

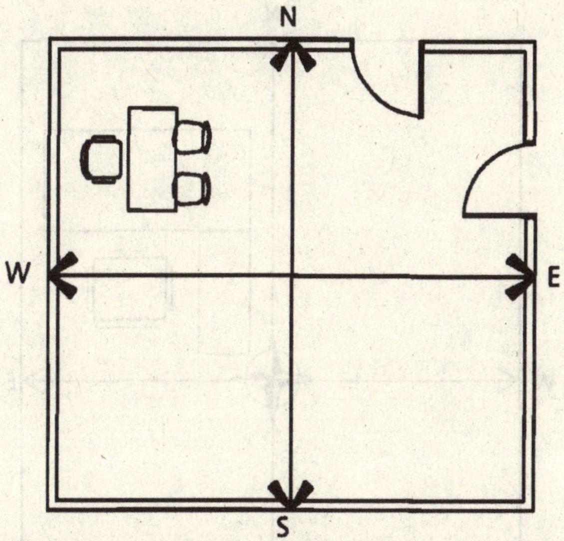

Location of the sales and marketing department

For the sales and marketing department the north-west is recommended.

Accounts

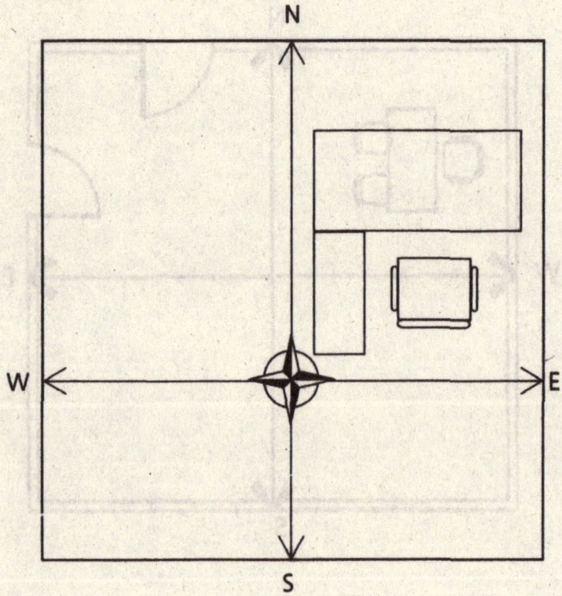

Location of the accounts department

In offices, the accounts department should be in the north. If there is an accountant, his work station can be located there. He should also work facing the north.

Administration department

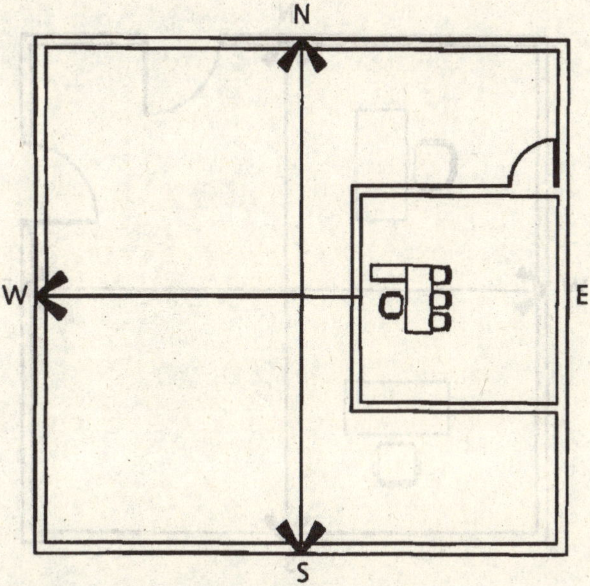

Location of the administration and personnel department

The administration and personnel department should be located towards the east. The head of the departments should also work facing the east.

Owner's desk

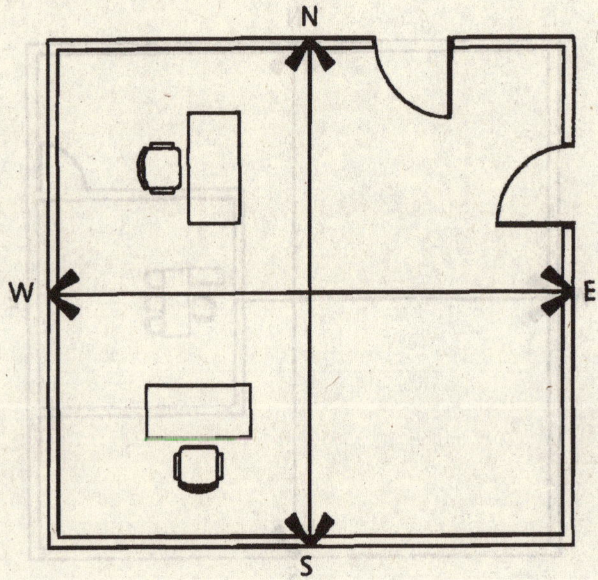

Sit facing east or north

The south-west corner should be used by the owner who should sit facing the east or north. However, if the entrance is in the south-west, the owner may sit in the north-west, which is also considered good.

Number of doors

Just as in a home, the entrance door of a shop or office should be viewed with sanctity. There should be no blockage of any kind nor any garbage at the entrance.

Shops normally have one entrance. However, a large office may have many doors. The important thing is that the number of doors should not be in multiples of 10, i.e., 10, 20, 30, and so on.

The number of doors can also be as per your own number, i.e., your date of birth. For someone born on 25-6-1940, (2+5) + (6) + (1+9+4+0) = 7+6+5 = 18 → (1+8) = 9 is an appropriate number of doors for a residence.

In the above case, the number of doors can also be an odd number other than 9. ***An even number of doors is unsuitable.***

Similarly, if your number is even, let's say, 24 -7-1971, → 6 + 7 + 9 = 22 → 2 + 2 = 4, the ***number of doors can be 4 or any even number except 10.***

Entrance door

Shops and offices facing the east and/or north are considered good.

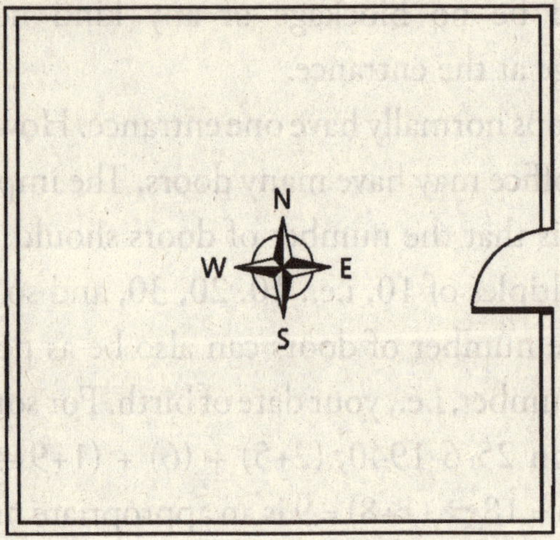

An east-facing entrance door

An east facing entrance door is auspicious.

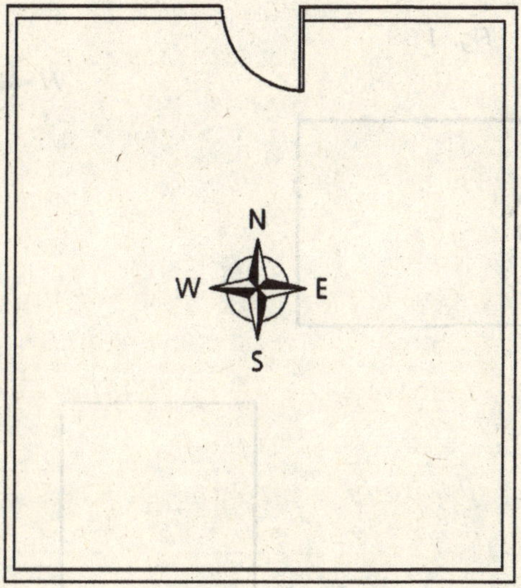

A north-facing entrance door

A north-facing entrance door is also good.

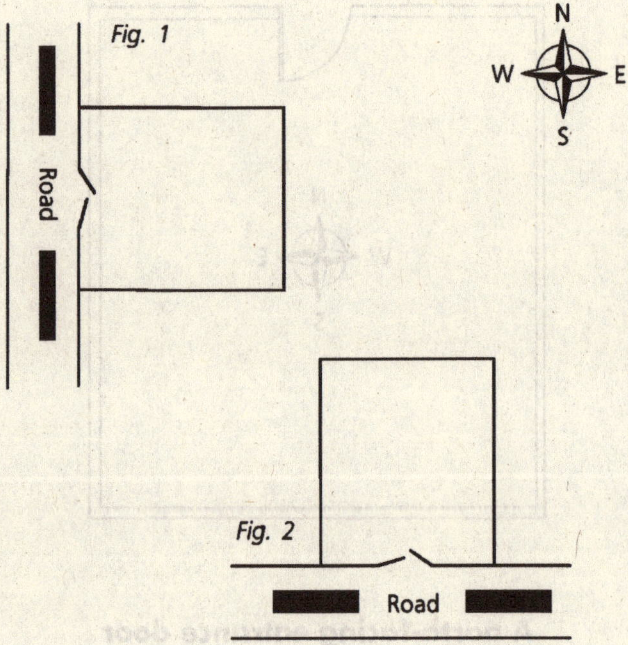

West and south facing entrance doors

Shops and offices facing west (as in Fig. 1) or south (as in Fig. 2) are considered good for the food and entertainment business.

Stocks

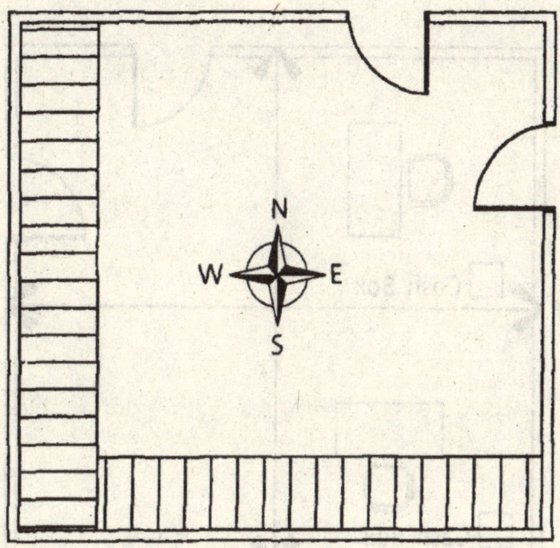

Position of stocks

Stocks should be kept along the south-west walls.

Safe/cash box

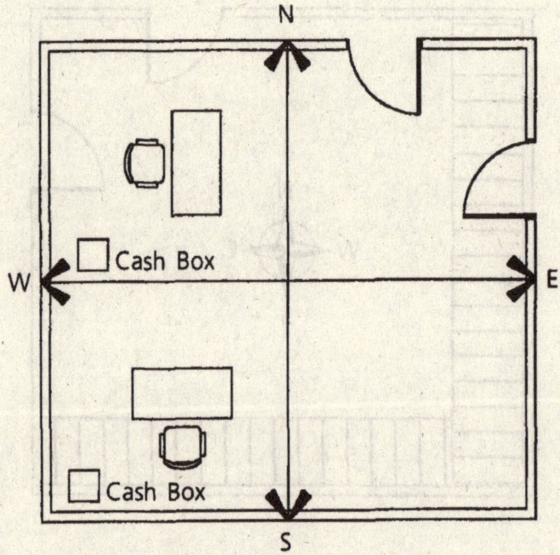

Position of the safe/cash box

If the owner or manager sits facing the east, the safe/cash box should be on his right. If he sits facing the north, the cash box should be to his left. In both cases, the safe is to open facing the north. It is not advisable for the owner to sit facing the south-west.

Puja room

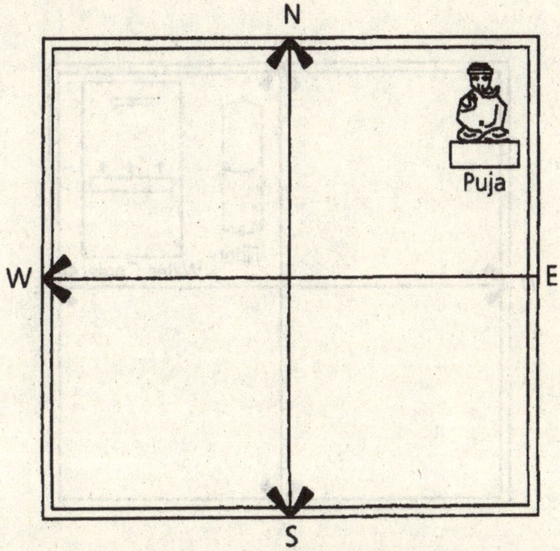

Location of the puja room

A small place for puja should be made in the north-east corner.

A water body

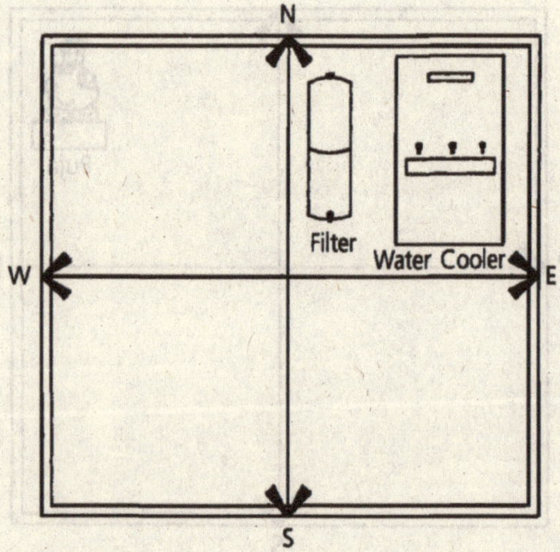

Position of a water body

In a shop or a small office, it is suggested that any water body, i.e. water container, water filter, or water cooler, be in the north-east quadrant.

Pantry/kitchen

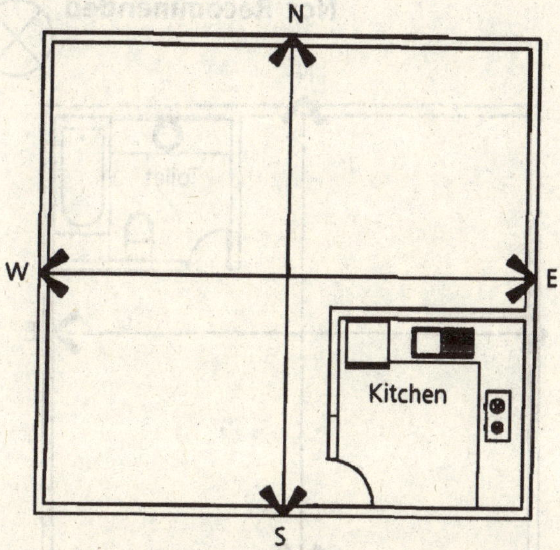

Location of a pantry/kitchen

A pantry, kitchen or even a heater in the south-east corner is considered good. However, note that a door in front of the stove, is to be avoided.

Toilet

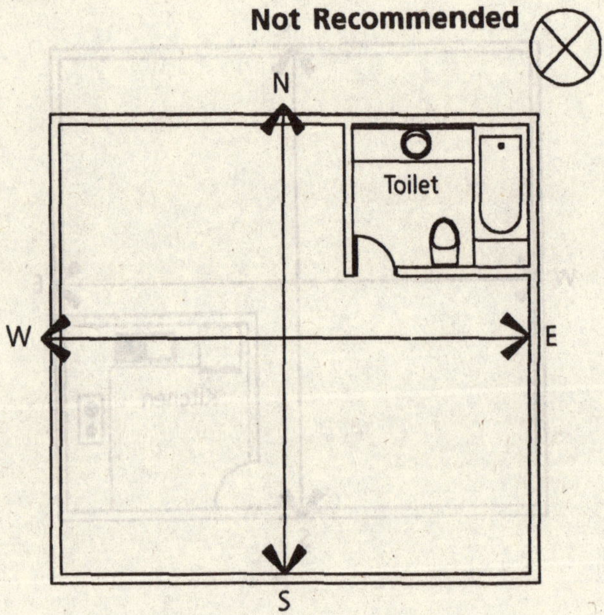

Location of the toilet

Whether in an office, shop or home, avoid having a toilet in the north-east or the south-west.

Staircase in office

Not Recommended

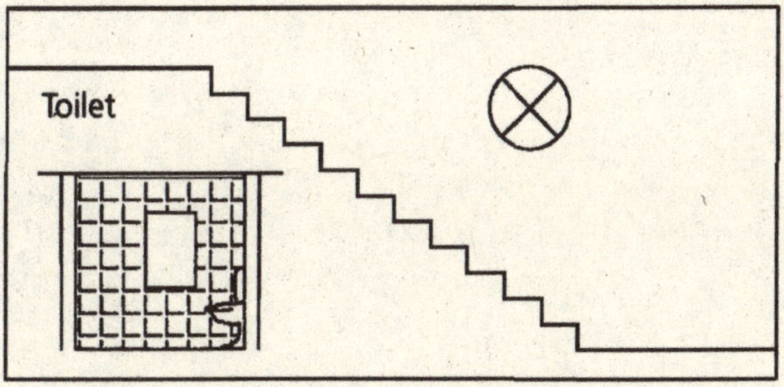

Do not keep a statue or have a toilet, or pantry under the staircase. As in homes, so in shops and offices, the staircase should be along the south-west wall as shown on pg. 84

Chapter Eight

EVALUATING SHOPS AND OFFICES

How to do the Evaluation Exercises

1. You will need a magnetic compass to do these exercises.
2. Start with Exercise 1. If, for example, your cabin is located in the west, circle 8 in the Points column.
3. Now turn to the Final Score Sheet on pg. 139 and write 8 in the column Your Score for Question 1.
4. Do the same for Exercises 2-10.
5. Now turn to the Final Score Sheet (pg. 139) and add your points. Write the Total.
6. See your rating on the Rating Scale (pg. 140).

Exercise 1

Where is your cabin or desk?

(See pages 110 to 114)

Location	**Points**
South-west	10
South	9
West	8
North-west	7
South-east	6
North	5
East	4
North-east	3

Exercise 2

Which side do you face while working?

(See pages 110 to 114)

Direction	Points
North-east	10
East	9
North	8
North-west	7
South-east	6
West	5
South	4
South-west	3

Exercise 3

Where is the safe/cash box?

(See page 120)

Location	**Points**
North	10
East	9
North-east	8
North-west	7
West	6
South-west	5
South	4
South-east	3

Exercise 4

Where is the sales department/counter located?

(See page 111)

Location	Points
North-west	10
North	9
West	8
South-west	7
South-east	6
South	5
East	4
North-east	3

In a small shop, where the owner sits in the south-west and conducts sales, the score can be reversed with the north-west, i.e., south-west will then score 10, and north-west 7.

Exercise 5

Where are the stocks kept?

(See page 119)

Location	Points	
South-west	10	(raw material)
South	9	
West	8	
North-west	7	(raw material)
North	6	
South-east	5	
East	4	
North-east	3	

For finished goods, just reverse the figure, i.e., for north-west show 10 points and for south-west 7 points. Normally, in small shops the stocks are all around the sales counter. There the stocks would mean finished goods.

Exercise 6

Which direction does the safe open?

(See page 120)

Direction	Points
North	10
North-east	9
East	8
South-east	7
North-west	6
West	5
South	4
South-west	3

For east-facing shops, the cash box is to be kept on the right. For north-facing shops, the cash box is to be kept on the left.

Exercise 7

Where is the pantry?

(See page 123)

Location	**Points**
South-east	10
North-west	9
South	8
East	7
West	6
North	6
North-east	4
South-west	3

Exercise 8

Location of the entrance door

(See page 116)

Position	Points
North-east	10
North	9
East	8
North-west	7
West	6
South-east	5
South	4
South-west	3

This applies only to shops and offices which do not have other shops and offices situated directly opposite to them.

Exercise 9

Where is the toilet?

(See page 124)

Location	**Points**
North-west	10
North	9
West	8
South-east	7
South	6
East	5
North-east	4
South-west	3

Exercise 10

The Floor level.

Note that this exercise also applies to situations where the building has split levels. The basic principles that apply to the slope of a plot also apply here.

Description	Points
Depression in north-east or elevation in the south-west	10
Depression in the north or elevation in the south	9
Depression in the east or elevation in the west	8
A level floor	7
Elevation in the south-east	6
Elevation in the north-west	5
Depression in the south-east/ north-west	4
Elevation in the north-east or depression in the south-west	3

Final Score Sheet for shops/offices

Exercises	**Points**	**Your Score**
1. Where is your cabin or desk?	10	
2. Which side do you face while working?	10	
3. Where is the safe/cash box kept?	10	
4. Where is the sales department/ counter located?	10	
5. Where are the stocks kept?	10	
6. Which direction does the safe face?	10	
7. Where is the pantry?	10	
8. Location of the entrance door.	10	
9. Where is the toilet?	10	
10. The Floor level.	10	
Total	100	

Rating Scale

Score	Interpretation
100	Excellent
80-99	Very good
51-79	Good
upto 50	Average

Chapter Nine

EVALUATING SUMMARY

Special care is to be taken while planning or redesigning the interiors of large projects. Though the basic parameters are the same, the flow of process, production, entrance and exit should be carefully designed. Since these structures can be complex, one should go in for need-based Vaastu to arrive at the right solution.

It is very difficult to get a good piece of property already built/constructed or vacant, which is absolutely Vaastu-right. Keeping the basic principles in mind, one can go on searching for something which fulfils at least the basic requirements of Vaastu, and make the appropriate changes. For any existing structure, such as your office, home or factory, one should not make structural changes simply after reading a book. In fact, structural changes in a building are like surgery on the human body, which a person undergoes only if the problem is very acute, and that too, only upon expert advice. Quite often, simply by changing the layout inside the house or office, one can achieve the positive or beneficial effects of Vaastu.

How to do the Evaluation Exercises

1. You will need a magnetic compass to do these exercises.
2. Start with Exercise 1. Assess the vibration you get. What did you score?
3. Fill that score in the Final Score Sheet on pg.154 against Question 1.
4. Do the same for Exercises 2-11.
5. Now turn to the Final Score Sheet (pg.154) and add your points. Write the Total.
6. See your rating on the Rating Scale (pg.155).

Exercise 1

Your feeling about the place

Assessment	Points
Very positive	8-10
Good	5-7
Average	3-4

If you get negative vibrations, either consult someone, or, if there is a choice, avoid the place.

Exercise 2

Any unnatural deaths or accidents

	Points
Yes	3
No	4-10

Exercise 3

Were earlier occupants happy or unhappy?

	Points
Happy	10
Healthy	9
Honest	8
Friendly	7
United	6
Unpleasant	5
Sick	4
Quarrelsome	3

Exercise 4

Was the previous owner successful?

	Points
Excellent	10
Prosperous	9
Slow growth	8
Average	7
In difficulty	6
In debt	5
Litigation	4
Failure	3

Exercise 5

Location of the front door or main gate

Location	Points
North-east	10
North	9
East	8
North-west	7
West	6
South-east	5
South	4
South-west	3

The above can change marginally according to whether the existing structure is residential or commercial, and if commercial, what is or was the activity.

Exercise 6

Position of the kitchen, boiler, furnace

Location	Points
South-east	10
North-west	9
South	8
East	7
West	6
North	5
North-east	4
South-west	3

Exercise 7

What is in the south-west?

A. *For a commercial space*

Department	Points
Office of CEO	10
Stocks	9
HRD	8
Sales	7
Computer	6
Conference Room	5
Accounts	4
Toilet	3

B. *For a residential space*

Room	Points
Master bedroom	10
Store	9
Drawing or dining room	8
Children's room	7
Guest room	6
Servant's quarter/garage	5
Kitchen	4
Toilet	3

Exercise 8

The staircase in homes and offices

Location	Points
In the south-west, turning clockwise	10
In the south-west, turning anti-clockwise	9
In the south, turning clockwise	8
In the south, turning anti-clockwise	7
In the west, turning clockwise	6
In the west turning anti-clockwise	5
In the north-west/south-east	4
In the north/east/north-east	3

Exercise 9

Tube-well/underground water tank in homes and commercial spaces.

Location	Points
North-east	10
North	9
East	8
North-west	7
West	6
South	5
South-east	4
South-west	3

Exercise 10

The surroundings

Description	Points
More open area in the north-east as compared to the south-west	10
Natural depression in the north-east	9
Elevation in the south-west	8
Good construction material used	7
Good neighbours	6
Not close to any public place	5
Pleasant front view, good facade	4
Your plot has lower prices compared to other plots	3

Final Score Sheet for existing structures

Questions	Points	Score
1. Your feeling about the place.	10	
2. Any unnatural deaths?	10	
3. Were earlier occupants happy?	10	
4. Was the previous owner successful?	10	
5. Location of front door or main gate.	10	
6. Position of the kitchen.	10	
7. What is in the south-west?	10	
8. The staircase in homes and offices.	10	
9. Tube-well/underground water tank in homes and commercial spaces.	10	
10. How are the surroundings?	10	
Total	100	

Rating Scale

Score	Interpretation
100	Excellent
89-99	Very good
51-79	Good
upto 50	Average

Chapter Ten

VAASTU FOR INDUSTRIALISTS

Vaastu considerations can deeply affect the prosperity of an industry. Given below are a few suggestions to draw positive energies to the workplace.

- It is very important that all areas of a factory be clean. To ensure this the CEO must regularly walk around the premises and see that high levels of cleanliness are maintained. If he notices anything that is unnecessary it should be disposed off soon.
- No by-products or waste products should be allowed to accumulate. They should be disposed off latest in a fortnight.
- The production flow should be south to north for metallic products, and west to east for non-metallic products.
- The production flow should preferably be clockwise rather than anti-clockwise.
- The factory should have a pleasing atmosphere, be well lit and well ventilated.
- The guard should face east or north, not south or west.
- It is auspicious to have a place of worship inside the premises towards the north-east.

- Most important, the well-being of the workforce should be kept in mind. They should be helped to relax with instrumental music in the workers' canteen, or with 5-10 minutes of simple exercises or deep breathing. This will help in removing tension and create positive vibrations.

Each worker should do 5 minutes of simple breathing exercise at any time of the day. He/she can even do it while working, as follows.

Inhale	Counting	1, 2, 3, 4
Retain	Counting	1, 2, 3, 4, 5, 6, 7, 8
Exhale	Counting	1, 2, 3, 4
Stop breath	Counting	1, 2, 3, 4

This simple exercise can be done for five minutes. It helps a person develop positive feelings towards himself as well as others.

Chapter Eleven

AN EVALUATION FOR INDUSTRIALISTS

How to do the Evaluation Exercises

1. You will need a magnetic compass to do these exercises.
2. Start with Exercise 1. Circle the relevant number.
3. Now turn to the Final Score Sheet on pg. 173 and write the number in the column marked Your Score for Question 1.
4. Do the same for Exercises 2-10.
5. Now turn to the Final Score Sheet (pg. 173) and add your points. Write the Total.
6. See your rating on the Rating Scale (pg. 174).

Exercise 1

Location of the main gate

Direction	Points
North-east	10
East	9
North	8
North-west	7
South-east	6
West	5
South	4
South-west	3

Exercise 2

Location of the production hall

Direction	**Points**
South-west	10
South	9
West	8
North-west	7
South-east	6
North	5
East	4
North-east	3

Exercise 3

Location of the quality control hall (in relation to the production hall)

Direction	Points
East	10
North	9
North-east	8
North-west	7
South-east	6
West	5
South	4
South-west	3

Exercise 4

Location of the underground tank/tubewell

Direction	Points
North-east	10
North	9
East	8
North-west	7
West	6
South	5
South-east	4
South-west	3

Exercise 5

Location of the heat source

Location	Points
South-east	10
North-west	9
South	8
East	7
West	6
North	5
North-east	4
South-west	3

Exercise 6

Storage of finished goods

Location	Points
North-west	10
West	9
South-west	8
South	7
South-east	6
East	5
North	4
North-east	3

Exercise 7

Storage of raw material

Location	**Points**
South-west	10
South	9
West	8
North-west	7
South-east	6
North	5
East	4
North-east	3

Exercise 8

Which direction do the CEO and production manager face?

Direction	**Points**
East	10
North-east	9
North	8
South-east	7
North-west	6
South	5
West	4
South-west	3

Both should preferably sit in the south-west quadrant of the plot.

Exercise 9

Where are the low lying areas?

Location	**Points**
North-east	10
North	9
East	8
All the same level	7
North-west	6
South	5
West	4
South-east/South-west	3

Low lying areas or depressions in the north-west, south-west and south-east should be filled up at the earliest.

Exercise 10

Where are the elevations?

Location	Points
South-west	10
South	9
West	8
South-east	7
North-west	6
North	5
East	4
North-east	3

The elevation at north-west should not be higher than at south-east. The elevation at south-east should not be higher than at the south-west. The elevations at north, east and north-east should be lowered at the earliest.

Final Score Sheet for Industrialists

Exercises	Points	Your Score
1. Location of the main gate.	10	
2. Location of the production hall.	10	
3. Location of the quality control hall.	10	
4. Location of the underground tank.	10	
5. Location of the heat source.	10	
6. Storage of finished goods.	10	
7. Storage of raw material.	10	
8. Which direction do the CEO and Production Manager face?	10	
9. Where are the low lying areas?	10	
10. Where are the elevations?	10	
Total	100	

Rating Scale

Score	Interpretation
100	Excellent
89-99	Very good
51-79	Good
upto 50	Average

CHECK-LIST

Are you facing any of these problems?

- *Union Problems.* Check the activities in the south-west (Earth).
- *Financial Problems.* Check the situation in the north-east (Water).
- *Litigation.* Check the situation in the south-east (Fire).
- *Sales Problems.* Check the situation in the north-west (Air).
- *Bankruptcy.* Check the situation at the centre (Space).

Chapter Twelve

GARDEN VAASTU

By nurturing plants and trees, we connect ourselves and partake of the harmony that pervades the cosmos. Vaastu always strives to underline our connection with the cosmos, and by being in touch with nature we pay obeisance to the forces of nature and the cycle of life.

A well maintained and planned garden is as important as a well-designed home, as it powerfully affects the occupants of the house. A pleasing garden adds to the vital *prana* or positive vibrations in your environment.

Garden Vaastu is simply a tool which enhances and channelizes these vibrations to the occupants of the house, and draws health and happiness towards them.

Start by making a scale plan of your garden. Mark the eight cardinal points — north, south, east, west, north-east, north-west, south-east, south-west.

Now see in which direction your garden lies in relation to your house. Remember, try to give your garden a regular shape. Square and rectangular gardens are the best. If there are any irregular parts it is suggested that they be filled with lights.

Good vibrations are created by a subtle blend of design, shape, proportion, colour and correct planting. With the appropriate use of pathways, hedges, screens, pergolas, shrubs, and walls, even a small garden can be subdivided into a patio, water garden, children's play area and vegetable plot.

And remember, colour plays a very important part in Vaastu, and the use of specific colours in each quadrant is prescribed. While the suggestions made here for plants and trees pertain to India, keeping the basic principles in mind, suitable plants and trees could be used in any part of the world. Selecting your plants in keeping with the prescribed colours for each quadrant would be a good way to proceed with planting.

Note that herbs and medicinal plants may be grown anywhere, as their healing powers bring positive energies. Similarly, plants that grow flowers which are used for *puja* may be grown anywhere.

Not considered auspicious are plants bearing thorns, such as cactus, and those that ooze milk, which are generally poisonous. Some plants are harmful for health, such as the *keora* plant (pandanus tectorius) which causes respiratory disorders. Very aromatic plants are best avoided as they attract snakes.

Auspicious trees are mango, coconut, *bel, neem,* betel, *champa, devdaru* (polyalthia longifolia), *chandan* (santalum allium), *mahua (*madhuca indica), *shaal* (shorea robausta). Trees can play a significant role in preventing misfortunes. The *ashok* (saraca indica) is one such tree.

Inauspicious trees are *imli* (jamirindus indica), *bargad* (ficus benghalensis) *pakaria* (ficus lucesus) and *peepal* (ficus religiosa). It may be noted that these trees are not inauspicious in themselves. They are prohibited from being planted close to a house chiefly because they are very large trees with deep and wide spreading roots which could damage the foundations of a house. They could also prove dangerous if they fell in a storm. Therefore, such large trees are best planted away from the house, or at the far end of a spacious garden or farm house.

The direction of your garden

- If your garden lies to the north of your house, have a prominent water feature in it.
- If it lies to the east of your house have plenty of fruit bearing plants and trees. This is because your garden would be receiving the early morning rays of the sun which are highly beneficial, and the fruits would thus be even more nutritious.
- If your garden lies to the south of your house, plant trees that are tall enough to block out the harmful ultra-violet rays of the mid-day sun.
- If it lies to the west of your house, tall trees and metal garden furniture would be most suitable. In some parts of the world there are strong westerly winds which the tall trees would protect against.

Garden design for each cardinal point

North. The north is associated with health and wealth. It is also associated with Mercury, which is represented by the colour green. Medicinal plants and herbs such as *tulsi,* coriander, thyme, and mint would be very auspicious. Money plant is also suggested.

South. Plant appropriate trees that block out harsh sunlight. The south is associated with Mars, so red or warm colours should predominate here, for example dahlia, rose, zinnia, nasturtium, poppy, phlox etc.

East. East, which is associated with growth and the sun, gets the rays of the morning sun, so be sure you do not have tall trees planted here which block these rays. If you get good sunlight in this part of your garden, colourful plants would do well here. The predominant colours should be golden yellow and green.

West. West is associated with Saturn *(shani)* and plants that are metallic white or pale blue, pale violet, grey or white, would do well. Silvery foliage would be right. The west could even contain a metal climbing fence for children.

North-east. The north-east is the most auspicious direction, and the zone of benevolence. Its element is water. This is the ideal place for a lily pond, a small pool or water body. *Tulsi* planted here would also be appropriate. Water in this quadrant is beneficial. Ideally, have a slight depression in the zone which will act as a reservoir for good energies.

North-west. Air is the element of the north-west. Flowers of the same colour may be used as for the west. Plant a tree whose movement you enjoy.

South-east. Fire is the element of the south-east. This is the ideal place to grow herbs and lush green foliage. Mint, fennel, and basil find favour in this corner. A citrus plant is considered very lucky.

South-west. In the southwest we propitiate the element earth. This would be a good place for a rock garden. Since it is also the area of power and relationship, you might have a sculpture of two human figures.

Centre. The centre is symbolic of the element space. Keep it clean and uncluttered, with perhaps some pots of *tulsi.*

Keep your garden clean. Do not allow dead leaves and twigs or any other junk to pile up there. It is your point for a communion with nature, so design your garden such that it brings you peace and joy.

Chapter Thirteen

VAASTU MEDITATION

I have always focussed on the strong connection between Vaastu and right living. To understand the effects of Vaastu on life we can compare life to a television set. There are times when the antenna of the set gets out of alignment with the relay station and the reception is disturbed. Similarly, in our life we can get out of alignment with our own true nature and with the nature of the world around us.

The disturbance within creates a disturbance in all spheres of our life. We are not in harmony with ourselves and not at peace with what is happening in our world. Our own picture gets distorted and we need to realign our antenna to catch the positive forces flowing in our direction. Vaastu helps to realign this antenna by removing the blocks which are hampering our quest for harmony and abundance.

However, once positive energies begin to circulate around us they need to be harnessed. We need to learn how to use these positive energies to change our lives. To be able to do this we need to have a peaceful frame of mind, and an ability to turn inward and stay focussed.

Meditation helps us do this. It is an everlasting source of power and energy which we acquire inside ourselves which sharpens both intellect and intuitive powers.

Suggested here are two meditations that complement Vaastu. Just as Vaastu balances the five universal elements in our surroundings, this meditation balances the elements within ourselves so that we feel a sense of harmony.

You may well ask, how is Vaastu meditation going to balance the earth, water, fire, air and space elements within us? The answer lies in the five lower chakras of our body, each of which represents one of the five elements.

The major chakras are seven in number and are centres of energy and consciousness which control the circulation of *prana* throughout the body. The spinal column supports the complex interconnections between the chakras. Each chakra activates a particular part of the brain and their harmonious cooperation provides the foundation for physical and psychic health as well as the human being's mental and spiritual evolution.

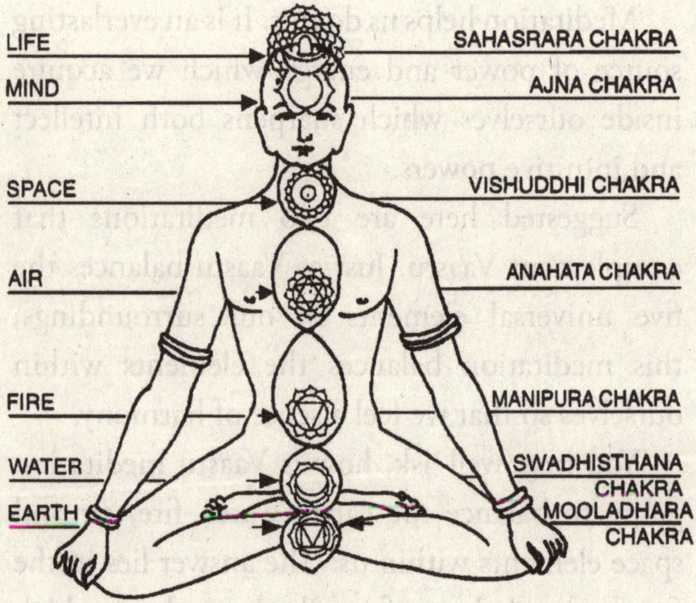

Behind the throat is the *Vishuddhi chakra*, which represents the *akasha tattwa* or the ether (space) element. It is the centre for sound.

The *Anahata chakra*, represents *vayu tattwa*, the air element. It is the centre for feelings of love and compassion. This chakra is associated with the circulatory and respiratory systems.

Located in the spine, behind the navel, is the *Manipura chakra*, the fire centre. It is the centre of the *agni tattwa* or fire element.

This fire is symbolic of the body heat centred

in the solar plexus, the region of digestion.

Directly behind the genital organs is the *Swadhisthana chakra,* the centre for *apas tattwa* or the water element. Though associated with sex energy, at a deeper level this chakra is the seat of the individual and collective consciousness.

Mooladhara chakra is the lowest of the chakras. *Mool* means rest and *adhara* means place. Therefore it is the root centre. It is the centre of the *prithvi tattwa* or earth element and is associated with the sense of smell. It is the seat of Kundalini shakti or primal energy.

The two higher *chakras* are centres of subtle energy. The *Ajna chakra* is situated in the mid-brain behind the centre of the forehead. Its element is *manas* or mind, and it is a centre where wisdom and intuition develop.

At the crown of the head is the *Sahasrara chakra*, the abode of highest consciousness.

TWO JOYOUS MEDITATIONS

Vaastu meditation

To get ready for the Vaastu meditation, find a suitable time, preferably early morning, though any other time will do as well. See that you are not disturbed for at least half an hour. It is pleasant to light an incense stick and not to have any bright, artificial light during the meditation. Lie on your back on a clean mat or blanket. However, if this is inconvenient, then simply sit comfortably in the lotus position, cross-legged, with your back and head straight.

Lie with your legs a little apart, hands on the sides, with palms facing upwards, or sit comfortably with your spine erect. Relax your body completely and try to remain absolutely still, calm and peaceful. Take a few deep, relaxing breaths, breathing in peace and breathing out all your worries. Feel the peace in every part of your being, as the worries leave you with each exhalation. Repeat the mantra "Om", three times.

Now visualise a golden light above your head

and feel the light coming down slowly towards you. Feel the light touching your head. Feel a tingling sensation, a vibration or simply a pulsation.

Bring the light inside your *Sahasrara chakra*, also called the crown chakra. Visualise your *chakra*, violet in colour, moving clockwise and anti-clockwise rhythmically, like the balance wheel of a wrist watch. Feel the chakra and know that it is there.

Now bring the light gently down into your *Ajna chakra.* Visualise the *Ajna Chakra*, indigo in colour, moving clockwise and anti-clockwise rhythmically. Feel your *Ajna chakra*. If any negative thoughts come to your mind, feel them leave like a grey cloud in the sky vanishing into oblivion. Feel the chakra getting brighter and lighter. Control the movement of the chakra with your breathing—clockwise when you inhale and anti-clockwise when you exhale.

Now let the light down into your *Vishuddhi chakra*, also known as the throat chakra. Visualise the chakra in front of you, blue like the sky, moving clockwise and anti-clockwise rhythmically. Feel your chakra. Feel negative thoughts leave your throat chakra like a grey cloud in the sky vanishing into oblivion.

Do not analyse or concentrate. Just do the exercise gently, with love and with faith. Feel the chakra getting brighter and lighter. Control the movement of the chakra with your breathing—clockwise when you inhale and anti-clockwise when you exhale.

Now, let the light come down to your *Anahata chakra*, also known as the heart chakra. Visualise your chakra, green in colour, moving clockwise and anti-clockwise rhythmically. Feel the chakra. Feel negative thoughts leave the chakra like a grey cloud in the sky vanishing into oblivion. Feel the chakra becoming brighter and lighter. Control the movement of the chakra with your breathing — clockwise when you inhale and anti-clockwise when you exhale.

Now allow the light to come into your *Manipura chakra*, also called the solar plexus chakra. Visualise the chakra, yellow in colour, moving clockwise and anti-clockwise rhythmically. Feel the chakra. Observe any feelings, thoughts or emotions that may come up. Feel negative thoughts leave the chakra like a grey cloud in the sky, vanishing into oblivion. Feel the chakra getting brighter and lighter. Control the movement of the chakra with your breathing — clockwise when you inhale and anti-clockwise when you exhale.

Now let the light flow down to your *Swadhisthana chakra*, also called the sacral plexus chakra. Visualise the chakra, orange in colour, moving clockwise and anti-clockwise rhythmically. Feel the chakra. Observe your mind and your feelings. Only observe. Feel negative thoughts or emotions leave the chakra in the form of a grey cloud rising into the sky, vanishing into oblivion. Feel the chakra getting brighter and lighter. Control the movement of the chakra with your breathing—clockwise when you inhale and anti-clockwise when you exhale.

Finally, let the light fill your *Mooladhara chakra*, also called the root or basic chakra. Visualise the chakra, red in colour, moving clockwise and anti-clockwise rhythmically. Feel the chakra. Feel any negative thoughts or emotions leave the chakra in the form of a grey cloud rising into the sky, vanishing into oblivion. Feel the chakra getting brighter and lighter. Control the movement of the chakra with your breathing—clockwise when you inhale and anti-clockwise when you exhale.

Now visualise all the seven *chakras* together, moving clockwise and anti-clockwise with your breathing. See the rainbow of colours, feel the rainbow, feel yourself to be a part of nature, in peace and harmony, moving in rhythm with the entire universe. All your *chakras* are balanced; all the five essential elements within you are in total harmony.

All your negative thoughts and emotions have been transmuted to positive feelings. You are fresh and revitalised. You feel as though life has just begun. Be in this state for some time.

Now slowly come back to consciousness of your surroundings. Take a few deep breaths, feel your body lying on the floor of your room or on your bed, and slowly move your fingers, toes, ankles and feet. Turn to your right and open your eyes. You may get up when you like. This completes the Vaastu meditation.

Earth energy meditation

Find a pleasant location close to nature—a garden, a beach, by the river or out in the open fields. Be relaxed. Just stand still and feel the sun shining its warmth on you.

Now start jumping and feel the sensation in your feet. You will soon feel the energy flowing through your legs, feet and down to the earth.

Now walk slowly and feel the energy flowing through your legs into the earth. After a few minutes of walking, stand bare feet, silently rooted to the earth, and feel a communion of your feet with the earth. A feeling of being whole and grounded will settle upon you.

You will observe that the earth communicates, and soon a dialogue between you and the earth begins. This meditation exercise helps you to communicate without using your ears and mouth. With this an unusual dialogue begins between you and your true self which makes you feel happy and fulfilled.

Chapter Fourteen

IMPORTANT SUGGESTIONS

1

The north and east are very auspicious directions as benevolent energies flow in from here. Keep the north-east corner of your home as clean and well-lit as possible.

2

A small water body (bird bath, aquarium, water tank, lily pool etc.) in the north, or east, or north-east brings prosperity.

3

Make sure no shadow falls on the front door as it can create many problems.

4

An auspicious symbol or image, such as Ganesha, is appropriate at the front door. The front door should be maintained and kept as attractive as possible.

5

In case your entrance door is directly opposite your neighbour's (as is often the case in apartments) make sure it is of a different colour or material.

6

The front door should not open to a dead wall. It brings many dead ends in professional life or in relationships.

7

Never have the entrance door opposite another door that leads out, as whatever comes in will as easily go out.

8

Note that the use of the Swastika symbol to position the main door (as explained on pg. 74), is in fact applicable for positioning any door anywhere in a building.

9

Do not have a trash can or rubbish heap in front of your main gate or entrance door.

10

Having *tulsi* or *neem* in or around the house is auspicious. Cactus or any succulent plant must be avoided. They create friction.

11

A toilet or tap in the centre of the house is considered very unlucky as it drains all the wealth away.

12

Repair any leaking tap. A leaking tap drains wealth away.

13

Avoid having the kitchen, toilets, and prayer room next to each other. These areas represent energies which should be kept apart.

14

The gas burner or the microwave in the kitchen should not be directly in front of the main door. This has a tendency to create stomach related disorders.

15

Never have a washroom or pantry under the staircase. It brings immense bad luck.

16

In washrooms, the mirrors, sinks and taps are best placed along the north or east wall.

17

The toilet seat should preferably be along the north-south axis. Numerous people worship the rising sun facing east hence avoid aligning the toilet seat east-west.

18

All electrical or heat generating appliances are recommended to be kept in the south-east, or at least their plug point (energy source) or the remote should be in this direction.

19

Your valuables, credit cards, cash etc. should be kept in a locker or cupboard which opens towards the north.

20

While vacuum cleaning your house remember to burn a candle at a safe place near the centre of the room to transmute negative energies.

21

To ensure that your educational career moves smoothly forward, study facing the east or north. Facing south or west should be avoided.

22

The oldest member of the house should be given the south-west bedroom. From oldest to youngest the bedrooms assigned should be in the south-west, then south, then west, then north-west, with the youngest member of the family being given the north-east room.

23

Never sleep or work under a beam. It creates health problems, starting with headaches.

24

Always sleep with your head towards the east or south. The head towards the west is acceptable, but it should never be towards the north. This creates a disturbance in the electro-magnetic currents of the body which manifests as blood pressure, cholesterol, and sometimes insomnia.

25

Never hang paintings depicting war, unrest, agony or distress as they release similar vibrations in the house.

26

Avoid keeping broken mirrors or window panes in the house. They cause many obstructions and are capable of breaking relationships.

27

The number of doors should not be in multiples of ten, and the number of windows should be more than the doors. In a double storeyed house, the number of openings in the ground floor should be more than the first floor.

28

It is recommended to taper the height of a building from south-west to north-east. Similarly, the walls along the south-west should also be marginally thicker than at the north-east.

29

Keeping an energiser in the foundation column is considered auspicious as negative energies get transmuted.

30

It is auspicious to perform the house warming (or *griha pravesh*) ceremony before occupying a house.

31

It is also recommended to do the prescribed ritual before you start construction. The beautiful prayer that is said on this occasion is given on page 24.